"RIGHT PROUD"

THE BUFFALO SOLDIERS

Martin Copeland

RAINBOW BRIDGE

CONTENTS

INTRODUCTION: IMAGINE A MOVIE

The story in this book was written as a feature film screenplay. Many readers, especially those unfamiliar with the form, may ask "why?"

The impression still persists that a script is little more than a blueprint for the director, a set of rather arcane indications, descriptions and dialogues that only he or she can interpret and transform into a motion picture.

In fact virtually all screenplays, especially those for feature films, are easily accessible to the general reader. They can be read and enjoyed on their own terms. The technical vocabulary that is used, necessary for the production team, consists of hardly more than a dozen terms. I have provided a Glossary of the most common in this book.

A big-screen feature film in a darkened theater with surround sound booming is such an impressive spectacle it can be difficult to realize all that sound and fury was created by a solitary soul or two writing in a room. But that is exactly what happens.

The proof is in the practice. Before a film can be produced it must be financed. In these days of $100+ million budgets, it is not a decision taken lightly. When the green light is given, most of the time it's for one hard and simple reason: the financiers have read and liked the script and believe in its commercial and/or artistic potential.

Equally they can commit because they like the "elements" attached to the project--usually stars or director. But why have these latter committed? 99% of the time because they too have read the script and been moved and excited. The screenplay is a definite literary form, another way of telling a story that makes full use of visual and sound elements... among others.

The historical Buffalo Soldiers roamed all over the ferociously arid Southwest, guarding stagecoaches, protecting ranchers, chasing renegades. And all that wasn't the half of what these neglected heroes did. Frederic Remington rode with the Buffalo Soldiers and left a priceless series of drawings of their daily life. Most of them are reproduced in this book.

In one, we see a squad of Buffalo Soldiers crouched on one knee in the middle of a firefight. We can almost hear the shouts and cries of battle, hear the gunshots. Almost, but not quite. For that, we need another medium than a still picture:

The black men--a troop of the U.S. 9th Cavalry known as the "Buffalo Soldiers"--have arranged themselves in a skirmish line, are crouching on one knee, taking aim with their rifles.

PANNING the Buffalo Soldiers as they wait, rifles poised. Their enemy is nowhere to be seen. All we hear is the sound of what seems distant THUNDER, growing louder.

THEIR POV

is of the wall of firesmoke billowing upward,
blocking their view of what's coming.
The THUNDER intensifies.

WRIGHT
Steady.

The soldiers are, as the drumming THUNDER peaks and--

Suddenly a phalanx of mounted Comancheros bursts
through the smoke as through a wall--a shattering,
shocking effect, the wall of smoke abruptly riven
by a mounted charge of shrieking Comancheros in
full cry, firing from their Winchesters, the horses
bearing down.

With masterful cool and precision, considering they
only have split seconds before the mounted charge
reaches them, the Buffalo Soldiers react.

GATEWOOD
Fire!

This scene would have been impossible to recreate
on the stage. It would have been perfectly possible
in a novel, but I doubt the novelist would have
made so much use of the firesmoke and thundering
hoofbeats. In a screenplay, one can make full use of
the resources of the film medium.

This story of the 9th Cavalry Buffalo Soldiers includes a relentless, tortuous gut march across infernal desert, a race up and down a cactus

mountain, a cat and mouse encounter with a sniper guarding a mountain pass, a climactic canyon battle

It works best as a movie, and that is how I imagined it.

In this book, the reader is invited to do the same.

GLOSSARY OF SCREENPLAY TERMS

EXTERIOR & INTERIOR--indicates whether the scene occurs outdoors
or in.

POV--Point of view. What a character sees.

PAN--camera movement. Can be as much as 360 degrees.

SERIES OF SHOTS--simpler term for montage.

INTERCUT--cinematic equivalent of counterpoint.

BEAT--slight pause.

IN FRAME--forefront of the scene.

ACT I

SUPERIMPOSE: 1879

EXT. DESERT - DAY (SUNSET)

Our view is a LONG SHOT past scrub and sand toward a distant CAMPFIRE. We can just hear VOICES and, at intervals, MUSIC.

A MAN'S SHAPE passes FRAME--squatting low, moving fast, indistinguishable--rustling scrub in the forefront of FRAME.

EXT. CAMPFIRE - DAY (SUNSET)

Music, laughter, song and dance. We're smack in the middle of a party. A young black man--ZACH BURLEY--is dancing around the fire, kicking up dust.

His friends seated around the fire egg him on with shouts and whistles. With one exception they are all black men, ranging in age from 18 to '40s.

ANGLE ON PINCKNEY

a young man strumming a banjo to beat hell.

ANGLE ON BODNEY AND JORDAN

keeping tune with Pinckney on harmonica and fiddle.

Raucous voices echo in the twilight: 'Do it, brother. Faster!' 'All right.' Etc.

ANGLE ON WRIGHT

an older man, CLAPPING, grinning at this exhibition.

WRIGHT
Look at that boy go!

He is. As the music builds to a wild end, Burley spins and whirls around the fire, dancing among the dust and sparks he kicks up--an effect that electrifies his audience even further.

On one of Burley's spins we PAN DOWN to pick up the lone white man in the group--GATEWOOD-- puffing his pipe, more sedate than the others. But he's clapping and nodding, enjoying the song and dance.

All the men are dressed in the mufti of the range. For all we can tell from appearances they might be the members of a traveling minstrel troupe, putting on a show for themselves.

The music builds, Burley dances like a dervish, and ends his dance as the music crescendos with a great spin, whirl and leap in front of his friends.

APPLAUSE from all except one, a tall man with long hair, half-black, half-Indian: SAM BOWMAN. He stares impassively with arms folded.

WOOD

a short man at his side, turns to him.

WOOD
You like that?

Bowman nods.

WOOD
Well clap your hands.

As he is doing--but Bowman maintains his impassive demeanor. Wood shakes his head, a little exasperated.

Burley takes his bows, then sort of struts and dances his way toward the bushes. Jordan does a light fiddle solo, improvised on the spot, to serenade his leavetaking.

ANGLE ON JONES

who has been enjoying the song and dance with particular pleasure.

JONES
Where you goin', Zach?

BURLEY
It's intermission.

A chorus of 'Naws,' groans and the like from the group.

Wood turns to the older man Wright, seated beside him.

WOOD
Intermission. What's that?

WRIGHT
You never been to a theater, boy?

WOOD
 (bravado)
Sure, lots of times.

Wright nods, skeptical.

WRIGHT
Comes between acts.

WOOD
What's a act?

Jones stands up in front of the group.

JONES
Y'all want to see some real moves?

A chorus of assent.

JONES
All right.

He launches into quite a dance, gyrating, swaying. The musicians pick up the tempo, improvise accompaniment.

BURLEY

looks back at the group he is moving away from, sees Jones.

BURLEY
Aw, what's that?

He laughs good-naturedly, moves on, farther out of the firelight--hears a SOUND. He stares, sees a creosote bush rustling--perhaps from the wind. He relaxes.

Burley unbuttons his fly, prepares to go about his business. He chuckles again, remembering the fun.

Suddenly his smile disappears.

HIS POV

A PAN upward reveals a tall, fierce-looking COMANCHERO. His rifle is scabbarded with bandolier, but he is holding a large knife. Burley stares hard at the Comanchero, whose stern visage betrays no emotion, no pity.

Burley does the unexpected--he smiles.

BURLEY
Caught me with my pants down, didn't you?

He chuckles. The Comanchero remains impassive.

BURLEY
Understand what I'm saying? Man can't pee and fight at the same time.

The Comanchero understands. Burley's merriment infects him, too. He cracks a smile.

BURLEY
You're gonna kill me, right?

The Comanchero nods, enjoying this joke, too.

BURLEY
Cut it clean off, right?
 (making a slicing gesture)
Whup!

The Comanchero nods again. Smiling wider, he
brandishes the knife to show Burley how well he's
imagined his fate. Burley's still laughing too--even
as, quick as an eyeblink, he whips out a
DERRINGER from his sleeve.

BURLEY
Wrong.

He shoots the Comanchero squarely in the
forehead.

EXT. CAMPFIRE - DAY (TWILIGHT)

At the sound of the GUNSHOT the rollicking group
instantly transform.

GATEWOOD
Now!

SERIES OF SHOTS

Wood shovels a load of dirt on the fire, creating a
wall of smoke.

The men who just moments before were clapping
and shouting hit the ground all together.

A FLURRY of GUNSHOTS ZING! into the campfire
region, and some ARROWS whip PAST FRAME,
embedding in the ground.

Pinckney turns on reflex as a COMANCHERO comes running into the firelight, war crying for a kill. Pinckney SLAMS him in the face with the banjo, knocking him out.

The men crawl into the shelter of an arroyo located just behind their campsite.

Gatewood hurls rifles, one after another, with amazing precision to the men.

A row of FLASHES signals a fusillade of rifle fire. Bullets SPATTER all around.

Bodney is hit as he flees for the arroyo. He yells in pain, falls wounded into the arroyo.

The Comanchero knocked out by Pinckney revives. Seeing the black men near at hand, he grabs his rifle and comes to his knees to snap off a shot, but before he can fire a man leaps down in front of him, barring his view.

It's Burley. He spins around--a great dance move-- wrenches the Comanchero's rifle away and shoots him with it.

Burley leaps into the arroyo.

Wright--his Sergeant Major--tosses him a rifle. Burley takes a position beside Jones.

GATEWOOD
Defensive line!

The black men--a troop of the U.S. 9th Cavalry known as the "Buffalo Soldiers"--have arranged themselves in a skirmish line, are crouching on one knee, taking aim with their rifles.

PANNING the Buffalo Soldiers as they wait, rifles poised. Their enemy is nowhere to be seen. All we hear is the sound of what seems distant THUNDER, growing loud.

THEIR POV

is of the wall of firesmoke billowing upward, blocking their view of what's coming. The THUNDER intensifies.

WRIGHT
Steady.

The soldiers are, as the drumming THUNDER peaks and--

Suddenly a phalanx of mounted Comancheros bursts through the smoke as through a wall--a shattering, shocking effect, the wall of smoke abruptly riven by a mounted charge of shrieking Comancheros in full cry, firing from their Winchesters, the horses bearing down.

With masterful cool and precision, considering they only have split seconds before the mounted charge reaches them, the Buffalo Soldiers react.

GATEWOOD
Fire!

As one--three Comancheros go down under the barrage.

The horses burst into, up and out of the arroyo. Two horses go down. Wright makes short work of one of the Comanchero riders, Jones the other. Jefferson SCREAMS as a shot from one of the riders' rifles grazes his shoulder. The rider is

AN APACHE

his long black hair tied in a bandanna.

JONES

fires at the Apache as he rides through. In the melee of dust and gunfire, he appears to wound him. The Apache struggles to stay in the saddle as his mount climbs out of the arroyo.

Jones gets up, pursues him for the kill.

BURLEY
Jones!

Too late. Jones is gone. Burley ducks as a barrage of gunfire from the Comanchers kicks up dust.

JONES

is pursuing the wounded Apache, who slumps in the saddle. His horse slows to a stop. Jones moves in for the *coup de grace*.

ANOTHER ANGLE

we see the Apache is holding to the reins securely. He jerks his horse around. Leaning down to ride sidesaddle, away from Jones' view, he races toward Jones.

JONES

his eyes widen as he realizes it's too late. The
Apache FIRES--

ANOTHER ANGLE

Jones is mowed down as the horse charges past.

The Apache rides a way, then pulls up next to a
Comanchero. We get a good look at this man.
Fearless, a master tactician and unquestioned
leader of the Comancheros, he is JOHN LOCO. The
hard riding young Apache at his side: his son
WASHINGTON.

Loco eyes the fighting. Now it is a series of fire
flashes from one side to the other, bursts of light in
the gathering darkness.

WASHINGTON
It was a trick.

JOHN LOCO
They learn from us.

DISSOLVE TO:

EXT. THE ARROYO - DAY (DAWN)

The soldiers tentatively leave their bivouac, climb
out into the desert. They see no sign of the
Comancheros. Burley scans the desert for signs of
Jones. Gatewood--the company's commanding
officer--and Wright--one of its sergeants--come up
beside him.

GATEWOOD
(softly, to Burley)
Lead a search party.

Burley nods, moves away.

GATEWOOD
Well, sergeant?

WRIGHT
We got two for sure. I'm guessing they
carried off a half dozen more.

Gatewood nods, relieved and pleased.

GATEWOOD
I call that a victory.

ANGLE ON PINCKNEY

He retrieves his banjo, notes the back is dented. He
turns it over. One string remains unbroken. He
PLUNKS it. Bodney and Wood come up, inspect the
body of the first Comanchero killed in the fight--the
luckless victim of Pinckney's banjo.

PINCKNEY
Look at this.
(holding up the banjo, to the
Comanchero)
Good thing for you you're dead.
(to Wood)
You reckon Mr. John Loco'll come back
for this boy?

WOOD
You kiddin'? He's runnin' again.

PINCKNEY
Lord, Lord.
 (eyeing the desert)
That means we'll be chasin'.

Again he PLUNKS the lone banjo string.

ON JEFFERSON

as Jordan bandages his wounded shoulder.
Jefferson holds up the bullet Jordan has dug out
for Gatewood to see.

JEFFERSON
Souvenir.

GATEWOOD
 (without pausing)
Add it to the others.

JEFFERSON
 (inspecting bullet)
Pretty soon I'll have me a necklace.

ON SAM BOWMAN

eyeing the ground, then peering toward the eastern
horizon. Gatewood comes up to him.

GATEWOOD
East?

Bowman nods.

GATEWOOD
Whole bunch?

Bowman nods again. Gatewood moves away, revealing Pvt. Wood IN FRAME, staring toward the same eastern horizon in puzzlement.

WOOD
(to Bowman)
I got good eyes. How come you see all that and I don't see nothin'?

BOWMAN
I'm taller.

He moves away, leaving Wood to puzzle over this.

DESERT

Burley and other soldiers are scattered around, searching for the missing Jones. Burley sees him first. Jones is slumped near a creosote bush, sitting up--but his head rests motionless on his chest.

ARROYO

Burley carries Jones back into the midst of the other soldiers and lays his injured friend gently down. Jones grimaces with each movement. He is clutching his stomach where a gaping wound has bled profusely through the night.

JONES
I got suckered.

BURLEY
You surely did.

Burley inspects the wound as the others--Wright, Gatewood, Wood, Bowman among them--gather round.

JONES
Ain't nothing. Patch me up and let's go.

He squirms a little as Burley checks the wound.

JONES
He rides a bay sorrel. Big man, carries a warclub.

ON WOUND

a ghastly sight--mixed dirt, blood, Jones' trembling hand trying to stanch a flow already occurred.

JONES
Leave him to me, understand? Next time he's mine.

BURLEY

swallows hard, tries not to show that from what he sees there may be no next time.

BURLEY
Understood.

EXT. DESERT (TRAVELING) - DAY

ON TRAVOIS

crudely built, being dragged behind Jones' horse. Jones, patched up as best can be done on the march, is lying on it, every jolt and shake paining him.

A WIDER ANGLE shows the troop on the move, heading east.

ANOTHER ANGLE

PANNING down from Jones' horse, emphasizing the desert dust they are marching through and kicking up--thick clouds of it, coating everything.

Jones is already covered with dust. As the horses top a bank, the dirt and dust swirl heavily, choking him. He coughs.

BURLEY

is riding beside his friend, watching him solicitously. Remembering.

FLASHBACK

INT. NEW ORLEANS HONKYTONK - NIGHT

We are in mid-song.

Belting out a verse of "Camptown Races" to beat hell is LADY BELLE. She's singing with all the heart she's got lots of, bouncing an outrageous body she's got lots of, too.

Acccompanying her is a young black man, HARRIS "LUV" HARRIS. His voice is mellow, beautiful.

The audience loves it, shouting, applauding, seconding. It is a black group, an even mix of women and men, who are there for Lady Belle's entertainment, maybe the best in New Orleans.

A piano player provides the musical accompaniment.

Lady Belle and Harris duo the last of the song and it brings down the house. APPLAUSE, SHOUTS, HUZZAHS.

Lady Belle hugs Harris, gives him a big kiss on the cheek.

LADY BELLE
Lordy boy, you sure can sing. What's your name?

HARRIS
Harris Harris, on account of my folks didn't have no imagination, but back home they call me "Luv."

LADY BELLE
Why's that?

He gives her a smile she can't mistake, bends down, tells it in her ear. Lady Belle laughs, slaps him on the shoulder.

LADY BELLE
Honey, round here sweet lovin' costs one dollar.

She moves off.

HARRIS
(yelling after her)
Well I ain't got it!

But hope resprings. He moves over to a henna-haired beauty, starts sweet-talking her.

BURLEY AND JONES

Enter the honky-tonk together. Jones is dressed
plainly, like the farm boy he is. Burley is a farm boy
too, but he is garbed like a riverboat gambler in a
flashy vest and big white hat.

JONES
What're we doin' here, Zach?

BURLEY
It's your birthday.

JONES
We can't do any celebratin'. We don't
have jobs or prospects. And we sure as
hell ain't got any money.

BURLEY
 (taking off his hat, massaging the felt)
Yet.

JONES
What'd you do, rob a riverboat?

BURLEY
Won it.

Burley smiles, shows a deck of cards stashed in the
bottom of the hat--ruffles a few for Jones' benefit.

JONES
Didn't know you were that lucky.

BURLEY
I'm good. Hal Jones, you're gonna'
remember this night as long as you live.

Watch me.

He heads over to a card table. Says to the players:

BURLEY
Gentlemen, I crave a game of skill and
chance.

They make him a place. Jones just shakes his head
at his friend's confidence, eyes him admiringly. But
when a BEAUTY comes up beside him, he passes to
other intentions. He spends a long moment
gathering courage--and then she smiles at him!
Jones is in heaven. He starts to say something--and
is abruptly elbowed aside by Harris.

HARRIS
She's smilin' at me, brother.

JONES
Says who?

HARRIS
Watch me.

He leans over seductively to the Beauty.

HARRIS
You believe in love?

BEAUTY
 (nodding)
Uh-huh.

HARRIS
Love don't have nothing to do with
money. It comes from the heart.

BEAUTY
 (nodding)
Uh-huh.

He leans down, whispers in her ear.

BEAUTY
 (shaking her head)
Huh-uh.

She turns away in a huff.

JONES
Whatever you said, don't tell me.

HARRIS
I ain't through. They don't call me Sweet
Lovin' 'cause of that heifer on
Grandaddy's farm.

JONES
Couldn't hardly go wrong here. All these
ladies are so pretty. And her--

He means Lady Belle. She sashays by, turning
heads, sparking dreams.

HARRIS
Lady Belle. It's her place. Every black
man in New Orleans'd like to watch the
moonlight with her. You got about as
much chance--
 (eyes him up and down)
Say, which bayou you from, boy?

JONES
How'd you know I was from the
country?

HARRIS
(a beat)
Counted the hayseeds.

The Beauty turns back. Harris motions for Jones to get lost.

HARRIS
Keep watchin', son.

Behind them, Burley lets out a WHOOP, rakes in a pile of winnings.

Jones smiles, happy for his friend. Suddenly Lady Belle lets out a joyous SHRIEK.

Sergeant Wright enters. Wearing the distinctive blue and yellow of the 9th U.S. Cavalry hat, he's an impressive figure and he creates an immediate wave of attention.

The girls in Lady Belle's flock toward him, including Harris' Beauty, who hangs him out to dry.

HARRIS
Hey!

Jones looks excited and intrigued as Lady Belle grandly greets the Sergeant.

LADY BELLE
A beer for the Buffalo Soldier!

SQUEALS and giggles from the girls. Lady Belle greets the sergeant with flamboyant hugs and kisses.

LADY BELLE
You've been away too long.
 (to the crowd)
Look how he's thinned out.

WRIGHT
Been livin' on lizards and horse piss.

The piano player hands the sergeant a mug of beer.
He seizes it gratefully, almost downs it all in one
huge gulp--a feat that brings "oohs" and "ahs" from
the crowd gathered around.

JONES
Damn.

Harris elbows his way in to the group, so as to be
closer to the Beauty who left him in the lurch. She
is his focus of attention, not the soldier. Jones isn't
far behind.

HARRIS
Come on, honey, forget Sergeant Bison.

JONES
 (to Harris)
Hey, what's a Buffalo Soldier?

Wright overhears. It's just the question he's been
waiting for. He mocks disgust, BANGS the empty
beer mug down on a table. The SOUND brings the
music to a halt.

WRIGHT
Hear that, Belle? What'd I tell you?
These boys shoulda stayed in the
cottonfields.

He strides forward, looking at the lot.

WRIGHT
Hell, I bet they ain't even heard of
emancipation. They ain't workin'. I can
tell that.

JONES
I'm lookin'.

Wright confronts him.

WRIGHT
Yeah. At the shoeshine stands. At the
stable, shoveling shit.
 (sticking his nose in Jones' face)
Sharecroppin'. Workin' like a mule and
gettin' treated a whole lot worse--you
hear what I'm sayin', boy?

The chastened Jones nods.

In b.g. Burley WHOOPS, rakes in the biggest pot of
all. The others give up; he's too lucky. They get up
from the table.

BURLEY
Hey, game's just getting good.

Wright circles around his now rapt audience. Jones
is listening to all this intently.

WRIGHT
Indians gave us the name, some say
'cause of our hair.

He tweaks one of his locks.

WRIGHT
Others say it's respect, 'cause of how we
fight. Buffalo's a sacred animal to the
Indians. That tell you something? We do
the job. We earn our money, $13 a
month.

GASPS from the crowd at this enormous sum.

WRIGHT
And a whole lot more. Satisfaction.
Honor.
 (fierce conviction)
Pride.

Burley comes up to Jones. Waving a pile of cash.

BURLEY
Look at that! Told you I was lucky,
didn't I?
 (looking around at the girls)
So what do you like?

JONES
Them uniforms. Means you're
somethin'.

Burley stares at him, incredulous.

WRIGHT
You want to know what a Buffalo
Soldier is? Find out for yourself.
Jackson Square Recruiting Station. U.S.
Cavalry. I'll be there. Waitin' to see who
wants to live for something bigger than
hisself.

Jones steps forward.

JONES
Sir--I'm with you.

The crowd buzzes. Some APPLAUSE, huzzahs for
Jones as Wright vigorously shakes his hand.

Burley looks stunned by his friend's decision.

JONES
I'm ready to sign up right now.

Under different circumstances Wright might take
him up on that, but he notices that the Beauty who
was Harris' quarry has also been moved by his
impassioned words. She is staring at him with
misty doe eyes--and she isn't the only one.

WRIGHT
Er, no, tomorrow morn--afternoon's just
fine. Like your attitude, son.

Wright shakes Jones' hand again, then turns his
attention to the Beauty. He circles his arm around
her and she's glad. Harris is aghast.

Burley buttonholes his friend.

BURLEY
You gone crazy?

JONES
 (wonderingly)
Can't hardly believe it. Black men in the
United States Cavalry.

BURLEY
Lot of black men in hell, too, but we
don't got to go there.

Burley shakes his head.

BURLEY
You need some educating. Quick.

He moves over, begins an earnest conversation with
Lady Belle. He uses his newly won cash to
punctuate the discussion.
Harris is still fit to be tied, but the Sergeant is
frying other fish than his Beauty at the moment. He
seizes the chance to sidle over to her and ask:

HARRIS
 (to the Beauty)
How come he gets the la-dee-da?

BEAUTY
Honey, he's a <u>hero</u>.

Harris doesn't need a picture--

HARRIS
 (loudly)
Count me in, sergeant!

Squeals of admiration from several of the girls.

HARRIS
 (emphatically)
Buffalo Soldiers, yeah!

More squeals. Wright comes over and shakes
Harris' hand, and one of the lady companions
kisses him on the cheek.

As for the Beauty, she looks at Harris with new eyes.

He's glad.

Jones is still watching the sergeant admiringly as Burley comes up.

JONES
I sure do like them uniforms.

Burley takes him by the shoulder.

BURLEY
Coupla' minutes from now you won't be thinkin' about nothin' higher'n your belly button. Jones my friend--

He wheels him around. There, hands on hips, smiling with a smile as wide as the Mississippi, is Lady Belle.

BURLEY
--you are about to become a man. Happy birthday.

He shoves him forward. Jones starts walking toward Lady Belle. He walks like a hypnotic, riveted.

Harris sees it all. Happy for his new friend, he signals to the rest of the crowd, then launches into a verse of "Camptown Races." Charged by his wonderful voice, they join in. As Jones walks toward Lady Belle, her wide smile and his manhood, awed and ecstatic at the prospect before him, almost the whole honkytonk is SINGING:

HARRIS & GROUP
 (singing together)
'Gwine to run all night,
'Gwine to run all day,
I bet my money on the bobtail nag,
Somebody bet on the bay.

EXT. DESERT - DAY

MATCH CUT

to Jones, on the travois. He is humming
"Camptown Races"--the theme song of the 9th
Cavalry--softly to himself. He turns his head with
effort to the side, eyes widening.

HIS POV

Soldiers are riding in a long line on the ridge above
them. It is another detachment of the Ninth, led by
MAJOR MORROW.

ANOTHER ANGLE

the soldiers head down toward them.

GATEWOOD

halts his troop and he and Sgt. Wright and Sam
Bowman wait at the head of the line for the arrival
of the other troops.

Morrow's troop has an ambulance wagon with
them.

GATEWOOD

salutes as Major Morrow rides up.

Luv Harris rides beside him.

MAJ. MORROW
Report.

GATEWOOD
John Loco hit us in force last night. We
did some damage. He's on the run
again.

MAJ. MORROW
Casualties?

GATEWOOD
Trooper Jones.

MORROW
Serious?

Gatewood nods yes.

Harris reacts to this news. He turns his horse and
we MOVE WITH him as he rides over to the travois,
dismounts. Burley is dismounted there beside his
friend as well. They exchange looks. Burley looks
grim and Harris reads the expression well.

Harris bends down beside Jones.

HARRIS
Hey, bunky.

JONES
 (to HARRIS)
Went and got myself shot, Luv.

HARRIS
Yeah, reckon you'll do anything to
impress the ladies.

JONES
 (chuckling)
Guess I ain't much of a soldier.

HARRIS
Hey, name me a great soldier who ain't
been nicked. I'm gonna recommend you
for a medal.

JONES
No jokin'?

BURLEY
Nobody's gonna give a medal to one of
us.

HARRIS
It's happened.

BURLEY
Takes an officer.

HARRIS
I'm an aide-de-camp, pretty much the
same.

Jones chuckles at this.

GATEWOOD AND MORROW

They have dismounted, are standing facing the
direction John Loco fled.

MAJ. MORROW
Your thoughts, Lieutenant.

GATEWOOD
He's heading to Mexico. He'll need water
even worse than we do.

Morrow nods assent.

MAJ. MORROW
Force march to Mimbres Spring. We'll
head for the waterhole at Alamosa.

GATEWOOD
Sir--

MAJ. MORROW
I regret the fact you're lugging a
wounded man, Lieutenant.
 (mounting his horse)
Take the wagon.

GATEWOOD
Thank you, sir.

Harris has come up beside them.

HARRIS
Permission to ride with Lieutenant
Gatewood, sir.
 (to Morrow's look)
Trooper Jones is my friend.

MAJ. MORROW
Granted.

He signals his men. The troop moves out.

AT THE WAGON

Harris joins Burley in lifting Jones into the back of the wagon.

BURLEY
Lie back easy.

HARRIS
Looks like I'm riding with you, Hal.

JONES
Careful. Stay with us, you're liable to meet some Comancheros.

HARRIS
So you shoot 'em and I'll break the news to their lovely wives.

GATEWOOD

waves the troop ahead.

GATEWOOD
At a gallop, forward yo!

ON JONES

grimacing as the wagon jolts into motion.

GATEWOOD

rides at the head of the column. Ahead we see the troop's destination: the Mimbres Mountains, a formidable arid range in the southern New Mexico desert.

FLASHBACK

EXT. LORDSBURG, N.M. TRAIN STATION - DAY

Clouds of steam and SQUEALING brakes signal the
arrival of the train to this remote New Mexico desert
stopover.

ANGLE ON WRIGHT

standing, waiting for the train to disgorge new
recruits.

ANGLE ON JONES

getting down from the train. He carries a tattered
bag, is dressed in wellworn clothes. He looks
around. Stepping down to join him on New Mexico
soil is Burley.

JONES
Looks good.

BURLEY
What looks good?

THEIR POV

PANNING the desert landscape: cactus, scrub, heat
waves coiling up from the sunbaked ground, mile
after mile of flat sand and dust immensity. The
pitiless southwestern desert.

PAN ends on Harris, who also has just alit from the
train.

HARRIS
Sheeit.

ON WRIGHT

WRIGHT
Army recruits! Fall in!

LATER - NEAR THE DEPOT - LORDSBURG, N.M.

The new recruits are lined up in front of Wright.
Burley and Jones and Harris--we also spot
Pinckney, Bodney and Jefferson--are among some
forty or so new men, some not all that young.

WRIGHT
From this point on, your asses ain't
your mama's, they ain't the white
man's, and they sure as hell ain't yours.
They belong to ME. I've never seen such
a sorry lot. Comancheros gonna pick
you clean, leave nothing but bones.
 (shoving his jaw in Harris' face)
You ever seen a Comanchero, boy?

HARRIS
No sir.

WRIGHT
You even know what a Comanchero is?

HARRIS
No sir.

WRIGHT
They're white men. Outlaws, bring
whiskey and guns to Indians, tell 'em
lies about us. Black soldiers, they like
to hang. Especially privates.

Wright pauses for emphasis.

WRIGHT
By their privates.

Harris' eyes widen but before he can even think about fainting they suddenly hear a COMMOTION. Eyes turn.

ANGLE ON HORSE AND HORSEMAN

future private Tyrone Wood is riding forward, if it can be called that. His bronc isn't quite broken, so it is alternately galloping and bucking its way toward the group. Wood is hanging on in the saddle, but a lesser rider would have been unhorsed long ago.

The horse charges in, then just as it reaches the group of recruits, begins to buck like hell. Wild hooves kick up dust and disaster.

BURLEY
Permission to retreat, sir!
Granted. Everybody scatters as the wild horse enters their midst, its lethal hooves shooting out like hammers. Wright takes cover along with the rest.

ANGLE ON WOOD

riding the bucking bronc, trying to tame it.

WOOD
Whoa!

The horse rears, its front hooves slashing the air, comes
down--and Wood hops off.

WOOD
Howdy.

The horse bolts off like a bat out of hell.

Wright has to leap out of the way again. Out of harm's way, he glares back at Wood, marches toward him loaded for bear. Wood is brushing the dust from his chaps as the others one by one come out from cover.

WOOD
Name's Wood. Looking to join the Army.
Ninth Cavalry.

He turns to Wright.

WOOD
Know where I can find an officer, Unc?

Before Wright can answer we HEAR O.S. the sound
of a window CRASHING, the horse whinnying and
the cries of panicked people. Wood just chuckles.

WOOD
Ain't broke yet, but I stayed on him all
the way from El Paso. Rattled my head
pretty good.

Wright shoves his nose in Wood's face--literally.

WRIGHT
I can tell.
 (a beat, glaring)
Look behind you, boy.

Wood does as Wright turns to the others:

WRIGHT
All you scrubs--take a look at some
soldiers.

They all turn eyes forward. Riding past them
toward the fort's training grounds is a company of
the 9th Cavalry--veteran Buffalo Soldiers.

INTERCUT COMPANY AND RECRUITS

the former standing tall in the saddle, militarily
erect, in perfect formation.

PANNING the recruits: with different measures of
respect and pride, they watch what they may
become.

END PAN on Burley and Jones. Burley looks
noncommittal. Jones' face is alive with anticipation
and excitement.

As the 9th Cavalry troop ride out of view, we

ANGLE ON GATEWOOD

who has just stepped off the train, the last
passenger to do so. At his side are his wife
CONSTANCE and sister NAN. Gatewood takes a
look around at the environs, then his wife.

GATEWOOD
(somewhat ruefully)
Well?

CONSTANCE
I expected worse.

She squeezes his hand for moral support. A
buckboard rattles up, a Buffalo Soldier at the reins.

INT. COL. HATCH'S OFFICE - FORT BAYARD - DAY

COL. HATCH is a distinguished looking man on
whom authority sits comfortably--a fact attributable
less to his much-honored military record,
experience and the bravery he has displayed under
fire, as to his natural qualities of leadership, justice
and fair play.

Hatch is pacing behind his desk, near a map of
southeast Arizona and southwest New Mexico.
Major Morrow sits to the side, near the standing
Gatewood.

COL. HATCH
The root of our troubles lies with the
Bureau of Indian Affairs. I won't tell you
what I think of that bunch. I've burned
Major Morrow's ears too many times. In
its boundless ignorance the Bureau
herded Victorio and his tribe onto the
reservation at San Carlos. Ever been to
San Carlos, Lieutenant?

GATEWOOD
No sir.

COL. HATCH
Go there some day.

MAJ. MORROW
In the summer.

COL. HATCH
You'll understand why Victorio wants to
live at Ojo Caliente, his homeland. John
Loco is a brigand, a damn good one, but
he doesn't know Arizona. When Col.
Gierson and the Tenth chased him out
of Texas we could have closed the trap
easy. But Loco convinced a band of
Victorio's best warriors to join him.
They know every cactus in this desert.
Thankfully Victorio didn't go along. If he
had--
   (a beat, musing, then turning back)
Well, the Army exists to enforce policy,
not make it.

MAJ. MORROW
And so far we haven't done a very good
job.

COL. HATCH
 (to Gatewood)
You volunteered for this regiment,
Lieutenant.

GATEWOOD
Yes sir.

COL. HATCH
Many white officers have refused, the
late George Armstrong Custer among
them.

GATEWOOD
I'm aware of that, sir. I'm also aware
that a white officer who serves with a
black regiment can expect more rapid
promotion.

MAJ. MORROW
A circumstance that might make you
question the caliber of our troops.

GATEWOOD
I prefer to withhold judgement on that.

COL. HATCH
Good policy.

GATEWOOD
We're facing a difficult situation.
Idealistic as it sounds, I think I can
help.

COL. HATCH
Well said.

Hatch moves over to the window, looks out.

HIS POV

Sgt. Wright is already drilling their new charges.

COL. HATCH
You'll find out soon enough about our
troops.

He comes over to Gatewood, extends his hand.
Morrow stands.

COL. HATCH
Welcome to the 9th Cavalry.

They shake on it.

BACK TO PRESENT

EXT. DESERT - DAY

On the march.

HARRIS

is at the reins of the ambulance wagon with Burley.

HARRIS
Hal.

JONES
Yo.

HARRIS
You reckon the Major's
missing me right now?

JONES
I betcha he's singing glory
hallelujah.

They share in laughter.

ANOTHER ANGLE

as we see the troop beginning to ascend a mountain
range.

THE WAGON

groans, creaks as it slows, the horses laboring
harder, the wagon tilting up the steep rugged trail.

BURLEY
Heading toward the sky, bunky.

ON JONES

in the wagon, jostling.

JONES
Gettin' closer to God.

EXT. WATERHOLE #1 - DAY

An ESTABLISHING SHOT shows several
Comanchero horses drinking long and greedily from
the watering hole, lapping the clear water.

ANGLE ON LOREN

a young, beautiful Apache woman, looking--not
exactly into the distance, but at some inner vision.
Her lustrous black eyes glow with the certainty of
revelation.

LOREN
They begin to climb the mountain.

JOHN LOCO

we now see has been standing near her. He is with
Washington and NANA, an aged Apache shaman.
Loco looks away from her and up toward a
promontory.

HIS POV

a SENTRY stands watch, his back to them. He gives
no sign for alarm.

LOCO
He doesn't see anything.

NANA
 (to Loco)
She sees beyond sight. Believe her.

Loco hesitates a beat, then barks a command to a
nearby group of Comancheros.

LOCO
Bring it!

THE HORSES

look up, startled, shift around in the water as the
sudden movement of men behind disturbs them.

WASHINGTON looks reflective.

WASHINGTON
They are different, these Buffalo
Soldiers. Others would rest. Not them.

JOHN LOCO
They have more to prove.

The Comancheros come up, lugging the carcass of a
freshly killed coyote.

John Loco brandishes a long hunting knife. As the
coyote is laid at his feet

CLOSE ON COYOTE

Loco RIPS open its guts with one swift, brutal
slashing stroke.

FLASHBACK

EXT. EQUESTRIAN TRAINING GROUND - DAY

A MONTAGE SERIES OF SHOTS of the recruits learning to ride in formation, progressing from

--A badly organized line of horsemen, woefully out of synch and line, to

--A helter-skelter of horsemen wheeling and turning, to

--A line of riders sauntering TOWARD CAMERA in finely tuned formation (reins in one hand, carbine in the other), then

--GALLOPING at full tilt, in formation, TOWARD THE CAMERA.

Throughout the sequence we see Wright on foot, barking orders; Burley, Jones, Pinckney et. al becoming progressively better riders; and

--Harris struggling. In the beginning he can barely manage to keep astraddle his horse; he flails awkwardly, holds the reins as if they were rattlesnakes; when he dismounts he holds his back and butt, walks away from his torturer horse like a cripple. He manages the final charge with carbine, but the rifle swings wildly right and left, at one point even drawing a look and duck from the rider at his side.

ANGLE ON MORROW AND GATEWOOD

strolling out to the grounds to observe, just as the troops make a charge with carbines.

MAJ. MORROW
Sergeant Wright runs "C" troop.

ANGLE ON WOOD

as the riders come to the end of their run they halt
in a solid, well-disciplined line, but Wood's got up a
head of steam. He roars past, WHOOPING, charges
toward a fence at the end of the training grounds,
sends his horse (the wild bronc, who has indeed
been tamed) leaping over the fence.

It's a spectacular stunt but as Wood wheels and
comes back to the group, Wright is fit to be tied.

Gatewood shakes his head at this sight.

WOOD

rides up to the troops, whips his leg around, leaps
off his horse in front of the steaming Wright.

WOOD
How'd I do?

Instead of answering, Wright starts circling Wood--
whose smile fades fast--and addressing the others.

WRIGHT
Hear that, gentlemen? Private Wood
wants to know how he did. He left
formation. Made himself an easy target.
Not that he'd be a big loss. But he
endangered you. Without discipline,
you're dead. Private Wood doesn't
understand that.

He leans down over the by now thoroughly subdued Wood.

WRIGHT
But he will.

INT. STABLE - DAY

PANNING the stable floor from the entrance, we see it has been scrubbed and picked and brushed clean, attributable we soon find to

WOOD

brooming vigorously in front of the stalls and singing while he works.

WOOD
(to the tune of"Camptown Races")
Gwine to sweep this straw,
Gwine to shovel this shit,
Bet your money on Pvt. Wood,
Don't you bet on the bay.

A horse in the still uncleaned area WHINNIES.

WOOD
Wait your turn!
  (gesturing at the cleaned stalls)
Understand? It's called discipline.

He goes back to his sweeping.

WOOD
Soon as I learn, I'll teach him.

He abruptly stops. A man is standing in front of him.

MOVING up from the boots, Wood gazes up, up--at Sam Bowman, the tall scout. Bowman gives Wood a look that betrays no emotion. He wordlessly moves into the stall behind Wood, begins checking on his horse.

WOOD
Hey, Long John. You an Injun?

No answer. Bowman busies himself with his horse. Wood moves closer.

WOOD
You don't look like a Buffalo Soldier.

BOWMAN
And you?

WOOD
I'm on special assignment.

BOWMAN
Careful you don't step in it.

WOOD
I know. You're a scout.

BOWMAN
Chief scout.

WOOD
So you're Apache.

BOWMAN
Half black, half Indian.

WOOD
Whoa, double trouble. What's your
name?

BOWMAN
Dzaneezi Ndee.

WOOD
Get serious. We're out shooting and
charging and I'm supposed to say,
"Cover my ass, Doozy day"?

BOWMAN
Black name, Sam Bowman.

WOOD
Yeah, Sam. Even a horse can pronounce
that.

Bowman starts to leave.

WOOD
You don't say much, do you?

BOWMAN
Better to talk little, say much. Sing like
bird, not squawk like crow. Hold
tongue, fill belly, think deep.
 (HEAR a PLOP O.S.)
Horse need you.

He moves away. Wood thinks a moment, but to all
that, what's there to say? He goes back to his
sweeping.

WOOD
Gwine to sweep this straw,
Gwine to shovel--

INT. BARRACKS - NIGHT

The men at ease--

PINCKNEY AND BODNEY

are working on a tune together, practicing the
sound they will later use around campfires and on
the trail. Bodney is playing harmonica and
PIinckney is softly humming various verses. Their
soft-hued melody fills the background as the men
move about their various tasks.

BURLEY AND JONES

Jones is carefully laying out his gear on his bunk.

BURLEY
What time is it?

JONES
Six, seven, I don't know.

BURLEY
Be about sundown in New Orleans.
Starting to cool off a little. People
coming out in the streets. Music
starting to play.

JONES
(nodding toward Pinckney and Bodney)
We got music here.

BURLEY
I'm talking nightlife.
Crowds, fun, good loving. Civilization.

JONES
Sergeant says we may encounter the
enemy soon. Better check your gear.

BURLEY
The only person dumber than you is
me.

ANGLE ON WOOD

bustling in with the scrub brush, broom, pail, etc.
he has been using to clean the stable.

JORDAN
Hey, it's the dog-rubber.

JEFFERSON
You remember to wash my horse? He
likes to be scrubbed behind his ears.
Like this. (exaggerated pantomime)

Laughter from them and other troopers quartered
near Wood, who busies himself stowing his gear--
carefully, orderly, patiently.

JORDAN
Mine's got fleas in his tail.
Pick em out for me, would you?

More laughter.

WOOD
You gentlemen got fleas for brains.

CLOSE ON LINIMENT

a thick, viscous concoction.

HARRIS

dips his hand in the goop, rubs his lower back--
gingerly--it's that sore. That done he carefully pulls
up his trousers over his hips.

Wright is busying himself nearby. He shakes his
head at Harris' discomfort.

HARRIS
We doing any riding tomorrow,
Sergeant?

WRIGHT
 (nodding)
Every day. Till that horse feels naked
without you.

Harris winces. He eases toward his bunk, delicately
arranges his pillow, sits--and leaps up. Even the
pillow is too hard. He grimaces, feels his backside
delicately.

WRIGHT
Why did you join the Army, Harris?

HARRIS
The truth, sergeant?

WRIGHT
The truth.

HARRIS
I heard the women out here looked like
angels and loved like devils. I'd have to
beg them to stop.

WRIGHT
What damn fool told you that?

HARRIS
You, sarge. (to his glare)
You'd had a few beers. All the women
I've seen out here look like beef jerky.

Wright shrugs.

WRIGHT
It's the sun. Dries em out. After a
couple campaigns you'll dry out, too.
And they'll look great.

He moves away.

HARRIS
Thank you, sergeant.

EXT. FORT GROUNDS - DAY

Wright and Gatewood are strolling, Gatewood with
his hands behind his back as if in an inspection
posture.

GATEWOOD
I've been watching the training
exercises. Frankly sergeant, these men
have a long way to go.

WRIGHT
Yes sir.

They pass Pinckney and Bodney, who are humming
harmony while they wait to take target practice.
Gatewood's look shows he finds their behavior not
the norm.

WRIGHT
We encourage the men to have a good
time, within limits. Eases tension.

GATEWOOD
Sometimes tension helps a soldier.

WRIGHT
Yes sir.

GATEWOOD
I brought along the latest Army training
manual. Your men should find it
instructive reading.

WRIGHT
Most of the men can't read, sir.

GATEWOOD
Well, read it to them.

Wright gives him a look. Gatewood gets the drift.

WRIGHT
By Army orders the regimental chaplain
is supposed to teach the men to read
and write. We haven't seen him in over
6 months.

Gatewood nods, a trifle exasperated.

GATEWOOD
We better hope John Loco stays in
Mexico a while longer.

EXT. SHOOTING RANGE - DAY

CLOSE ON TARGETS - SERIES OF SHOTS

Straw flies from tops, sides and bottoms as a
BARRAGE OF BULLETS hit the haybales and
sometimes the target, but never the bullseye.

PANNING the row of riflemen, we see all the recruits
in the process of loading, unloading, firing their
Springfield carbines at the targets.

WOOD

is attempting to fire in synch with the riflemen at
his side. Wright leans over.

WRIGHT
Private Wood.

WOOD
Sir?

WRIGHT
On the firing line you don't need to
maintain formation.

WOOD
Yes sir!

Wood nods gratefully. Now Wright looks
exasperated.

HARRIS

is firing willy-nilly.

ON HIS TARGET

it is unscathed.

JONES

is aiming his carbine carefully. He FIRES.

THE SHOT

hits very close to the target. Three other shots have
come close as well.

Jones smiles. He turns to Burley at his side.

JONES
You gonna join the party?

Burley raises his rifle with the practiced skill of one
who knows very much what he is doing, aims, fires.

HARRIS

is still rapidfiring.

THE TARGET

is still unscathed.

HARRIS
Shit.

Wright has been observing. He leans down.

WRIGHT
You ever use a rifle before?

Harris shakes his head.

WRIGHT
 (pointing at the gunsight)
It's called a sight. Before you shoot,
aim.

Accepting this revelation, Harris tries again--this
time aiming.

HIS SHOT

hits near the bullseye.

HARRIS
Hey, makes a difference!

Wright nods--more exasperated. He stands erect.

WRIGHT
Cease firing!

He moves out to confront the men again.

WRIGHT
We got work to do here. That was the
worst--

He notes Burley lounging nonchalantly, not
listening.

ANOTHER ANGLE

as Wright goes jaw to jaw with Burley.

WRIGHT
How did you do, private?

BURLEY
Square hit. Sir.

WRIGHT
 (gesturing at target)
Private Wood.

Private Wood goes running down to check the
target. When he gets there his eyes widen.

WOOD
Bullseye!

A stir, rumble from the other troopers.

BURLEY
Used to hunt with my grandpa.

WRIGHT
A fox squirrel don't shoot back. Do it
again.

Burley again takes aim--hesitates. Wright has stuck his pistol barrel against Burley's head, to simulate pressure.

WRIGHT
It's not loaded--I <u>think</u>. When you hear
the click--

Burley nods. There is a bead of sweat on his brow. All the other recruits have stopped everything to watch.

Wright releases the hammer. CLICK! Burley fires. Wright turns, looks at the target.

WRIGHT
Missed it clean.

BURLEY
 (calling Wood)
Check the hole!

Wood does so. His eyes widen again.

WOOD
It's bigger!

Louder rumble from the troopers. Burley can't help but smile.

Wright glares.

WRIGHT
 (to Burley)
If you'd hit it square, that
hole'd be the same size.

Burley's smile disappears. Wright turns to the others.

WRIGHT
Everybody back on the line, now! I want
to see some shootin'!

LATER

ANGLE ON MAJOR MORROW

at a makeshift desk set up out doors under a shade
tree to beat the heat. He is signing papers as
Harris--holding his back and backside--hobbles up.

HARRIS
Private Harris, sir.

MAJ. MORROW
Something wrong with your back,
Private?

HARRIS
Nothing a brisk hard ride in the saddle
won't cure, sir.

MAJ. MORROW
I like your sand.

HARRIS
Yes sir, I'm a real firebrand.

MAJ. MORROW
What can I do for you, private?

HARRIS
I hear you're looking for an aide-de-
camp.

MAJ. MORROW
That I am.

HARRIS
Like to respectfully volunteer, sir. Your
wish will be my command. I'll be the
best aide you ever aided.

MAJ. MORROW
A firebrand like you, I should think
you'd miss combat.

HARRIS
Dreadfully. But it won't do for the Major
to be missing an aide-de-camp.

MAJ. MORROW
Quite right. We'll give it a go.

HARRIS
 (beams)
Thank you, sir.

MAJ. MORROW
And don't you worry, you'll see some
action. I like the frontline. My last man,
poor devil, got cut off in our brush with
the Mescaleros. They spreadeagled him
on a cholla cactus. Wouldn't ask for
mercy, so they started cutting him up,
slow, big chunk pieces. Never breathed
a word. What guts. Hard to imagine a
braver man. Trust you're cut from the
same cloth, private.

Harris is stupefied, but he doesn't have to respond as a MESSENGER suddenly rides up, leaps off his horse with an urgent message for the major. Morrow reads it rapidly, springs up.

MAJ. MORROW
John Loco's crossed the border. Saddle
my horse, on the double. Looks like
you'll get that brisk hard ride, private.

He moves away, leaving Harris nonplussed.

HARRIS
Thank you, sir.

BACK TO PRESENT

EXT. MOUNTAINSIDE - DAY

The Buffalo Soldiers, ambulance wagon creaking in the rear, continue their ascent of the mountain. In the wagon, Trooper Jones endures the wagon's rumbling and shaking as best he can.

72

EXT. WATERHOLE #1 - DAY (DUSK)

MATCH CUT

WRIGHT
Easy now.

The troop is approaching the waterhole. It is eerily
serene and quiet in the setting sun.

BURLEY
(at wagon reins, looking back at Jones)
Gonna get you a drink, Bill.

The troopers ride slowly forward, scanning all
around for an ambush. They get closer and closer
to the waterhole, see nothing.

Several men WHOOP at this, hop off their horses
with their canteens, run toward the waterhole.

GATEWOOD AND WRIGHT

spot something beside the waterhole, react
simultaneously. They pull their revolvers, fire off a
barrage of shots that SPLATTER the water beside
the troopers before they can drink. They halt.

WRIGHT
That water is poisoned!

Almost as one the troopers see what Wright and
Gatewood see:

THE COYOTE

eviscerated.

Wright moves over to the coyote, kneels down. Lifts up the gashed stomach, showing where the sodden entrails have been dragged across the pool of water. The trail across the water is discernible.

WRIGHT
There's an acid inside. If it doesn't kill you, you'll wish it had.

The men stare forlornly at the waterhole--a lovely sight, but now utterly useless to them.

PINCKNEY
Thank you, Mr. John Loco.

BURLEY

comes around to the back of the wagon, peers inside.

Jones is lying inside. His wound has festered, the bandage a mass of dried blood. Flies BUZZ around it.

BURLEY
Gonna have to wait a little longer for that drink.

JONES
All the pain's gone. I don't feel nothing. That's good, ain't it?

Burley's look betrays the truth that it isn't.

ANGLE ON WRIGHT

WRIGHT
Mount up, now!

FLASHBACK

EXT. FORT BAYARD - DAY

The 9th Cavalry in formation, preparing to move out. A rush and jumble of mounted men and horses, shouted orders.

JONES

is in full field uniform, his gear strapped to his saddlebags, carbine attached to his side. He is armed and ready. He exchanges a look with the rider at his side--Burley. They say nothing.

GATEWOOD

gives his wife a goodbye kiss, bids farewell to her and his sister. He strides away from the officer's quarters toward the waiting troop.

ANGLE ON WRIGHT

jockeying his horse back and forth in front of his men. He edges over to Wood.

WRIGHT
Keep your line, trooper.

ANGLE ON MORROW

striding out to his horse, whose reins are being held for him by Harris. Morrow takes them from him, mounts, eyes the waiting troop.

MAJ. MORROW
 (to HARRIS)
I ride hard and fast, private. Stay close.

He gallops toward the front of the regiment.
Grimacing in pain, Harris mounts his horse. The
horse spins, rears, Harris regains control.

HARRIS
Shit.

He gallops toward Morrow.

ANGLE ON COL. HATCH

standing, watching the troop pass before him. He
raises his hand in salute as the men move past.

THE TROOP

ANGLING ON various of the principals--in
particular Wood, who is doing his damnedest to
stay in formation.

LONG SHOT - THE REGIMENT

moves out from the fort toward the horizon.

ACT II

EXT. ENCAMPMENT - NIGHT

GATEWOOD

is inspecting the horses in the remuda. Flanks, hooves. He shakes his head at what he finds.

BURLEY, JONES AND HARRIS

are hunched in a circle playing cards. Their pot: nickels, dimes and some tobacco.

HARRIS
I'm gonna' scare the life out of you when
I show down this hand.

JONES
Don't need any persuadin'. I'm out.

BURLEY looks at his hand and quietly rejoins:

BURLEY
You might scare me, pard, but you can't
scare the fixins' I got here.

Harris lays down his hand. It's a good one all right,
but Burley's is, well--

HARRIS
Shit!

AT THE CAMPFIRE

Wood is pounding open tin food cans for the mess.

WOOD
Got to look on the positive side. Ain't
everyone's a dog-rubber. Makes me
special. "Tyrone Wood, dog-rubber."
Yeah, I like it.

But as he looks inside one of the cans, he doesn't
like what he sees and EXCLAIMS in disgust.

WOOD
Sergeant!

INSERT CAN

the hardtack crackers inside are infested with
weevils.

LATER - ON WRIGHT

WRIGHT
You got something against weevils?

WOOD
Yes sir. They're ugly little bugs.

WRIGHT
So, spit 'em out.

WOOD
You mean the U.S. Army expects us to
eat this shit?

WRIGHT
 (softens)
That's standard provisions--for us.

WOOD
Tell you the truth, I ain't real hungry.

WRIGHT
Sorry, son.

Wright gives him a sympathetic pat on the
shoulder, moves away.

Gatewood has come up, overheard this
conversation.

Gatewood moves over to Wright who has reached
into the mess area and picked up a can of
provisions for himself.

GATEWOOD
I'll get that changed.

WRIGHT
It's been tried.

Gatewood thinks a moment.

GATEWOOD
Those horses are the scrawniest lot I've
ever seen at a major cavalry post.
Standard?

Wright gives him a look that says it all. Gatewood
looks toward Wood, still at his unappetizing task.

WRIGHT
One thing though. The bullets they give
us work just fine.

EXT. MCCRAE RANCH - DAY (DAWN)

The ranch--a large spread with many corrals and a
large main house--is under attack.

ANOTHER ANGLE

various COMANCHEROS circle around and through
it, whooping in the excitement of a pillage. Many
are lugging away the ranch's possessions.

EXT. HILLSIDE

ANGLE ON WRIGHT'S TROOPS

lined up in perfect formation, waiting to charge.

PANNING THE TROOPERS

each in various stages of prefight emotions. Most
look nervous, a mix of excitement and
apprehension. Wright maneuvers in front of the
troop.

WRIGHT
You men signed up to become U.S.
Cavalrymen. Now's your chance.

Jones is mounted beside Burley.

BURLEY
Well, you happy now?

JONES
I'm gonna do good. See if you can keep
up.

CLOSE ON HAT

Wood's. He is adorning it with an array of rabbit's
feet and feathers. Sam Bowman watches, impassive
as usual.

WOOD
 (to Bowman)
My good luck charms. Every one's been
blessed by a gypsy, shaman or gospel
preacher. Whoever shoots me ain't
getting into heaven.

Gatewood and Morrow are watching the horizon. In
a moment they get their signal: a rifle shot. Morrow
signals.

The BUGLER blows CHARGE.

As one, the troopers barrel downhill. As they ride,
we notice Wood doing his best to maintain
formation.

ANOTHER ANGLE

We now see the regiment has been split into three units. They are converging in a triangle on the farmhouse.

AT THE RANCH

the troopers converge en masse, revolvers drawn, ready to engage the Comancheros--and find nothing. The warriors have vanished.

The troopers mill about on their horses. Major Morrow dismounts, leads other officers on an inspection tour of the ranch. They find no sign of the warriors.

JONES

is reining in his lively horse. He has a position in back of the ranch. He is watching the officers check out the ranch.

Suddenly he HEARS footsteps, looks quickly to the side, sees a Comanchero running past him--rifle raised for a quick shot at Jones.

Jones instantly FIRES, hitting and killing the Comanchero.

Jones' shot unleashes the entire Comanchero raiding party. They go riding out of the bushes near Jones.

He YELLS to signal the rest of the troop, fires off a couple shots at the fleeing Comancheros.

Wright and the other leaders head their squads in pursuit.

MAJOR MORROW

watches them go.

EXT. PASS - DAY

as Wright and Gatewood, riding at the head of the troops, signal a halt. They look around for a trail, having lost sight of their quarry. They are in a field of house-sized boulders.

Suddenly SHOTS ring out all around them, shattering off the rocks, spraying fragments.

Two troopers are wounded. They fall off their horses. Gatewood signals the troop to dismount and take cover. They do so as a fusillade of SHOTS SPANGS around them.

The soldiers return fire--heavy, intense and frequent.

WRIGHT

notices Gatewood crouched down beside a boulder, firing with his rifle.

WRIGHT
Lieutenant, you'd be safer <u>behind</u> the
rock.

Gatewood notices he is indeed firing from an exposed position. He scrambles behind the boulder.

GATEWOOD
Well said, sergeant.

WRIGHT

observes that most of the enemy fire is coming from a particular point in the rocks above them.

WRIGHT
Let's hit that breastwork.

Wright points at it.

Several soldiers take aim.

WRIGHT
Now!

A fusillade from the troopers BARRAGES the rocks. We see the movement of Comancheros behind. The boulders are BLASTED by the intense fire. After a moment of this, Wright signals a halt. They see no more movement--until we see the Comancheros scrambling behind the boulders, and the SOUND of horses galloping.

Silence.

HARRIS

stands up slowly. A bullet BLASTS beside him. Then as other men peek out from behind their cover, more BLASTS hit the rocks.

HARRIS
 (to his fellows)
You heard the sergeant, stay down!

He gives them the example.

Wright scopes out the scene.

WRIGHT
(to Gatewood)
One man guarding the pass.

GATEWOOD
Let's rush him.

WRIGHT
Ain't that easy, sir. He's moving around,
he's a crack shot and he's got position.

Gatewood peers over the rock. A bullet BLASTS
beside him, just missing.

GATEWOOD
I see.

Wright thinks a moment, then turns.

WRIGHT
Private Burley!

LATER

Burley slips a fresh cartridge into his carbine. He is
standing near Wright and Gatewood.

WRIGHT
You'll have a split second.

Burley nods, looks over toward his friend Jones,
who is hunkered down behind a boulder.

BURLEY
Draw his fire.

Jones nods, takes his rifle, extends the barrel above
the rock. The Comanchero's shot BLASTS beside it.
Burley stands, whips his rifle toward the quick blur
that is the marksman, FIRES.

The marksman ducks behind a rock a second
before Burley's shot SLAMS into it.

WRIGHT
Too slow.

Burley reloads again with a look of determination,
snaps the breech shut forcefully.

JONES
 (to Burley)
I'll fix him.
 (yelling at sniper)
Hey, asshole!

Jones jerks down his pants, sticks out his butt
from behind the rock and MOONS THE SNIPER!

ANGLE ON MARKSMAN

for just a second as stunned by this as Jones' fellow
troopers--just long enough for

BURLEY

to stand and snap off a shot.

THE MARKSMAN

is hit. He plunges down from the rocks.

The soldiers watch the fall--then raise a CHEER.

Burley is surrounded by the men, clapping him on the back for congratulation.

Burley and Jones embrace, pat each other on the back for a job well done, smile happily.

WRIGHT
(to Burley)
Next time get him with the first shot.

Burley is taken aback, but not for long as Harris and Wood come up and as in b.g. Gatewood turns to Wright--

GATEWOOD
(to Wright)
The men fought well.

--the group of enlisted men move away together, joshing.

HARRIS
Wasn't the bullet killed him, it was seeing your ugly ass.

JONES

on his face is a smile wide as the Missouri.

BACK TO PRESENT - MATCH CUT

Jones is smiling at the memory as he lies on a pallet of blankets spread on the ground beside the campfire.

EXT. CAMP - NIGHT

Pinckney has jerry-rigged the banjo so it now at
least stays together. He is plucking a tune on it--
light, but on the one remaining string, it somehow
has a touch of melancholy to it.

This is the deathwatch but the men are trying not
to show it. They move about the fire as if going
about their normal business. But their
conversation is studied, strained. Burley keeps vigil
beside his friend.

GATEWOOD

is standing with Wright and Bowman. They speak
softly.

GATEWOOD
How far is this spring?

BOWMAN
Many miles.

GATEWOOD
If we ride like hell, we might beat him
there.

BOWMAN
Might.

ANGLE ON JONES

trying to lick his lips, caked with dust and alkali.

JONES
Tongue's dry as this dust.

With abrupt resolution Burley stands up, moves over to his horse, unstraps his canteen from the saddlebag.

Burley starts to move over to Jones. Wright grabs his shoulder.

WRIGHT
We still got a desert to cross.

BURLEY
I'll make it.

WRIGHT
He won't.

BURLEY
That's why.

Wright takes his hand away. Burley moves over to Jones.

BURLEY
Gonna wet your whistle, Hal.

He shakes it. The sound is negligible. Almost empty.

Burley grimaces--but before he can bend down to give his friend a drink suddenly there's another canteen held out to him--by Harris.

Burley gives him a thankful look as Harris pours a few precious drops of his water into Burley's canteen.

Then it's Wood's turn. Pinckney's.

Burley accepts them all with gratitude.

A last man adds his small contribution: Sgt. Wright. Burley looks surprised.

The canteen fuller now, Burley bends down, puts the canteen to Jones' mouth.

BURLEY
Here you are, bunky.

Jones takes it gratefully. As he finishes the drink, he smacks his lips.

JONES
That was good. Thanks.

He looks at all of them gathered around.

JONES
Everybody's here. Ought to have a
party. Your voice still work, Luv?

HARRIS
I reckon.

JONES
Like to hear it.

HARRIS
You got it.

Harris pauses for just a moment, then begins his song

HARRIS
(sings)
Well I looked over Jordan—

--his voice breaks. It's a moment before he can continue. When Harris finds his voice:

HARRIS
(singing)
Well I looked over Jordan
And what did I see,
Comin' boy to carry me home, A band of angels comin' after me, Comin' boy to carry me home.

Jones is relaxed in reverie.

JONES
He sings good. Better than the angels. Up there in Glory Land they're lookin' down and saying, son, hang on till we hear that boy sing. Well all right. All right.

He looks down at the jacket he has been using as a blanket. Rubs the cloth.

JONES
Sure messed up this uniform. Reckon I can get another?

BURLEY
(fighting emotions)
Whatever you want, soldier.

JONES
I'm real proud of it.

Assured, Jones leans back, his eyes open, staring toward the sky.

JONES
Real proud.

He says no more.

Wright takes the jacket from the dead man's hands
and lays it over his face. All bow their heads as
Harris' song rises richly melodious toward the
heavens.

HARRIS
 (singing)
Swing low, sweet chariot,
Comin' boy to carry me home,
Swing low, sweet chariot,
Comin' boy to carry me home.

DISSOLVE TO:

EXT. GRAVESITE - DAY

Jones' newly dug grave. A crude cross marker has
been erected at its head. The wind is already
scattering the dust from the upturned dirt.

BURLEY

is standing beside it, staring numbly at the resting
place of his friend.

In b.g. we see the troop riding out, the desert dust
rising in their wake.

After a moment Burley mounts, rides slowly after
them.

EXT. DESERT - DAY

The troopers' horses labor through an area of sand dunes. One horse, cresting a dune, loses its footing and falls, sending its rider tumbling off into the sand. No one pauses to help as the trooper scrambles through the deep sand toward his struggling horse.

LATER

the men are trudging beside their horses. Both show in look and attitude the rigors of their forced march. On the men's faces is a mix of dust and dirt, caking hair, lips, eyes-- almost masking them. Their conversation is hoarse, throats rasped by sun and sand.

HARRIS

is trying to lick the dust from his lips--but most of it remains.

HARRIS
 (to the trooper at his side)
Can't spit no more.

WOOD

notices his horse urinating. He is walking near Wright and Harris.

WOOD
Before long I may want to drink that.

WRIGHT
I've done it.

Wood thinks about this a moment as they trudge along.

WOOD
How did it taste?

WRIGHT
Wet.

ANGLE ON BURLEY

just standing, staring off into the desert. His face is begining to be covered with windblasted sand. His expression is empty and vacant as the landscape, a mirror of his emotions.

WRIGHT (O.S.)
Burley!

The voice brings Burley out of his reverie.

WRIGHT
Mount up.

Burley notices the column has mounted, is moving out on horseback. Burley nods mechanically, climbs onto his horse.

EXT. WATERHOLE #2 - DAY

The waterhole rests at the base of a cliff. It is clear, fresh, no traces of a coyote or anything else to mar its oasis-like quality.
PANNING from the waterhole around the area--a rock-strewn depression, capturing the runoff from the heights above.

END PAN on Sam Bowman, his rifle cocked, on advance scout. Satisfied the area is clear, Sam turns to shout toward the waiting troop, but his throat is so dry he can't form the words.

ON KERCHIEF

Sam's, as he dips it in the water, holds it up and squeezes some of the precious liquid down his throat.

ON TROOP

waiting, Gatewood and Wright at the head. They see Bowman mounting a boulder, waving.

BOWMAN
Whooeee!

The troopers stir, start to move forward, their thirst threatening to conquer their discipline.

GATEWOOD
Rout step yo!

He waves the troopers forward. They shout--as best they can--and gallop forward en masse.

AT THE WATERHOLE

it's a thundering herd!
The troopers ride pell-mell forward, leap off and plunge into the water. Men and horses greedily gulp the lifesaving water. Splash happily. Shouting with joy and newly refreshed spirits.

BURLEY

rides up slowly, the last of the men to arrive. He
gets off his horse, moves over to the waterhole.
Kneels. Painfully removes hat and bandanna,
bends down to drink.

Burley eyes the rippling water, a lucent reflector of
the cliff above.

IN THE REFLECTION

a BOULDER--falling!

In the blink of an eye Burley knocks the man at his
side-- Harris--out of the way.

The boulder CRASHES into the pool, just missing
Harris but crushing another trooper.

More boulders follow an instant after, crashing into
the pool now become a death trap.

The troopers scramble for cover.

BURLEY

in a rage seizes his carbine from off his horse,
starts scrambling up the cliff slope as fast as he
can make it. His face is contorted with rage.

Wright directs a group of troopers in a fusillade of
rifle fire at the positions on the cliff where the
boulders have come from.

But there is no more movement, no sound. After a
moment Wright signals to the men to cease firing.

The men come out from cover, eyeing the cliff warily. Still no sign of movement. Wood, Pinckney and Jefferson move over to the pool.

Their comrade's body floats in the pool. His blood is spreading across the water, dyeing the surface with crimson.

Gatewood motions to the body.

GATEWO0D
Get him out.

The troopers move over to the waterhole beside the body and lift it up, move it out to the ground. In their wake is a pool now thoroughly stained with blood.

GATEWOOD
Fill your canteens.

The troopers look at him as if he's crazy. Gatewood stares back at them, understanding their revulsion. But--

GATEWOOD
If you want to live.

ON THE CLIFF

Burley reaches the top, a viewpoint where he can see all the clifftop and desert below. He looks around for signs of the Comancheros. Sees none.

BURLEY
John Loco!

His shout is lost in the winds.

BURLEY
John Loco!

No answer. He aims his rifle, fires a shot at a spire
of rock. The bullet PINGS off uselessly.

BURLEY
Come out and fight! Just you and me.
John Loco!

The shout echoes off the cliff.

A hand grabs Burley by the shoulder, startling him.
It is Wright's. He points toward the desert below,
where a column of dust signals the escape of John
Loco and his men.

WRIGHT
Mexico.

EXT. NEAR FORT BAYARD - DAY

Gatewood and Wright's units straggle into the fort,
looking very much like the spent soldiers they are.
Clothes, faces, gear all reflect the tortuous--and
futile--campaign just waged.

Gatewood is riding beside Wright.

GATEWOOD
We need a new strategy. You got any
ideas, sergeant?

WRIGHT
Just one, sir.

But before he can voice it a column of the 6th
Cavalry rides by. They are a marked contrast to the
9th. The soldiers are all white. Their uniforms are
clean, mounts fresh, spirits unbowed by recent
combat.

They ride by the 9th soldiers jauntily, eyeing their
bedraggled condition with curiosity and some
condescension.

In particular we notice a handsome young officer
near the head of the column: LT. HARVEY SMITH.

As the column passes:

WRIGHT
 (to Gatewood)
That's how it looks.

Gatewood gives him a querying glance.

WRIGHT
Clean.

EXT. JOHN LOCO'S STRONGHOLD - DAY

John Loco is hoisting a young Apache child high in
his arms; tossing him. The child laughs excitedly.

Loco shares the joy, smiles. All around is a hubbub
of meal preparation.

WASHINGTON

is cleaning his rifle, discussing tactics with a
Comanchero while the Apache women prepare a
sumptuous meal--made with captured provisions.

LATER

John Loco addresses the group. He aims his words
particularly at the members of the Apache tribe.

JOHN LOCO
You joined me because the white men
took away the free life you loved. So we
take away their food.

This brings laughter from the group.

JOHN LOCO
You paid for it with your
blood and the lives of your children.
Enjoy it.

He sits down. While the others dig in with alacrity,
he waits a moment, looks reflective. Exchanges a
look with Washington.

FLASHBACK

EXT. SAN CARLOS RESERVATION - DAY

The reservation's INDIAN AGENT--a burly, bearded, brutal man--is supervising the doling out of provisions to the reservation Indians.

Nearby we see two Apache police lolling in the shade.

LOREN

eyes the quantity of food he has just received. She looks around.

The Indians are greedily eating the food as soon as they receive it.

Loren approaches the AGENT, who is mopping his brow in the torrid heat.

LOREN
My uncle Nana suffers in the heat. Give
me another to take to him.

AGENT
One per customer.

LOREN
He is our medicine man.

AGENT
Just another Injun to me.

Loren turns, looks at Washington, and we see him for the first time here. His hands are tied high to a post so his toes just rest on the ground by the barest of purchases. Another cord wrapped around his neck virtually garrots him.

Loren takes another look at the scant amount in her tin. That and the spectacle of Washington embolden her.

LOREN
You have no right to keep him like that.

AGENT
He half killed one of my police. Had a
dog like him once. Mean. Sooner die
than lose his pride.

He reaches in a bin, tosses some grains of corn at Washington's feet.

Washington doesn't deign to look at them.

AGENT
I strung him up just like that and when
he got real hungry--well, now he licks
my boots. And likes it.

The Agent moves over to Washington.

AGENT
How about it, breed? You ready to beg?

Washington doesn't even react. The Agent gives him a brutal kick in the balls.

Washington gasps, chokes, spits--

The Agent smiles.

Loren tosses her tin of food in the Agent's face. He splutters, rages, grabs her by the hair, wrenches--

AGENT
You're gonna join him.

He wrenches her around but something makes him go stockstill--

A MAN AND A KNIFE

big, a Bowie--in the hand of John Loco. He packs two guns, has a bandolier and a rifle slung over his shoulder.

The Agent looks for help from the Apache police, but sees they have been disarmed and are bracketed by two burly Comancheros.

Without a word, Loco turns, SLASHES the cords holding Washington who falls in his arms.

Loco eyes him for a moment--the ordeal of no food and water for many days shows on Washington's face. He cannot speak. Loco turns him over to a Comanchero.

The Agent's bravado disappears, fast. He lets Loren go.

She backs away.

AGENT
(to Loco)
What's he to you?

LOCO
I gave this boy life.

AGENT
You kill me, you'll have hell to pay.
From the U.S. government.

LOCO
People like you--my people--took away
everything in life that made him a man.
You got any idea what that is? Like
when you want to say so many things,
and can't get out a single word. You
talked some real wickedness. Words of
hate.

He suddenly grabs the Agent by the hair, jerks his
head back, thrusts the Bowie knife in the Agent's
mouth--gouging out his tongue. The Agent
struggles futilely, would scream--but just like that,
he no longer can.

EXT. RESERVATION - DAY

Washington is finishing a long drink from a boda
bag. The cool water revives him. He is standing with
Loco on a slope, looking down at the reservation.

WASHINGTON
I would like to burn this place.

JOHN LOCO
 (softly)
What happened to her?

WASHINGTON
White man's sickness. Their medicine
could do nothing.

JOHN LOCO
We had some good days together. Some
luck she had, falling in love with a white
man, outlaw to boot. She wanted to
keep you away from all that. She was
right.

WASHINGTON
Their yoke is too hard. I am finished
with peace. If you stay in this land, you
will need help. Many will follow you,
father. I will be the first. Sinetauka.

Loco says something in Apache. The words visibly
move Washington.

He embraces his father. They hug warmly.

EXT. OUTSIDE RESERVATION - DAY

Standing beside their horses as the band of
Comancheros move out, Loco and Washington
watch as, trailing behind, is a procession of young
Apache warriors.

Behind them come Loren, her aged uncle Nana,
and some elderly Apache women. Loco looks
askance at these last, but Washington reads the
look and has an answer:

WASHINGTON
Good cooks.

BACK TO PRESENT

EXT. JOHN LOCO'S STRONGHOLD - DAY

Loco watches as these same aged Apache women serve the repast to his united band of Comanchero and Apache. Loco takes a tin, smiles when he sees the stenciled lettering: "U.S. Government."

INT. GATEWOOD'S QUARTERS - DAY

Newly shaved, freshly scrubbed, reclothed in a
clean uniform, Gatewood is checking the new man
out in front of a mirror. He brushes his hair back
with his hands, heaves a happy sigh of
contentment. In b.g. his wife Constance is reading
from a local newspaper.

CONSTANCE
(reading)
"John Loco has been crowned Emperor
of North America. The people of Arizona
heartily concurred in the coronation, as
it is now clear John Loco rules all areas
of the American West. The United States
Cavalry was invited to attend the
ceremony but became lost in the desert.
Emperor Loco sent his compliments."
They're trying to be funny.

Gatewood shakes his head at what he has heard.

GATEWOOD
Now I know why I didn't miss the
newspaper while we were gone.

He comes over, hugs her.

GATEWOOD
You're a different story.

He begins kissing her.

INT. BARRACKS - NIGHT

WOOD
"Emperor of North America." Bullshit.
We chased his ass all over Arizona and
New Mexico. Who could have done
better?

BODNEY
6th Cavalry. Least that's what they
think.

JORDAN
Why else you think they're here?

Wood thinks a moment.

WOOD
Bullshit.

ON HARRIS

studying himself in the mirror. Pinckney sits on his
bunk beside him, idly plucking a ditty on his one-
string banjo.

HARRIS
 (rubbing his cheeks)
Pinckney, am I drying out?

Pinckney looks at him, puzzled. He keeps plunking
away at the banjo.

LATER

Harris along with Wood, Jefferson, Bodney and
several others, are getting dressed in their best
civilian clothes.

Sgt. Wright passes them, heading out himself, but he is dressed in full uniform.

WRIGHT
You gentlemen heading into town?

HARRIS
(straightening his suspenders)
How could you tell?

WRIGHT
Watch yourself. Some places, we ain't welcome.

He exits the baracks.

BURLEY

hears the sergeant's words. He has been glaring at Pinckney, still plunking on his banjo. Suddenly he leaps to his feet.

BURLEY
(to Pinckney)
Dammit man, the thing's done for!

He slips a finger under the banjo's string, BREAKS it with a quick flip. The string BOINGS as it snaps.

BURLEY
What's wrong with you people? A man's dead. Rotting out in that stinking desert. For what? This.

He holds up his Army issue blue cavalry shirt.

BURLEY
This.

HARRIS
Let it be, Zach.

Burley stares at him for a long moment, torn
between rage and contempt for the object he holds,
then angrily tosses it into the barracks stove. The
flames greedily welcome it.

Burley stalks out angrily. The others watch him go.

EXT. APACHE INDIAN RESERVATION - DAY

A fierce Apache WARRIOR is IN FRAME. Tall,
muscular, lean, looks as if he could run a hundred
miles without sweating. Naked except for a
breechcloth, he is regarding two riders coming into
the encampment. They are

GATEWOOD AND WRIGHT

at slow gait, passing the daily life of a proud tribe
now beginning to degenerate in this dusty arid
patch of land good for nothing except to banish an
unwanted race.

Gatewood and Wright observe around them curious
children, defiant young men, suspicious elders,
arrogant uniformed Indian police watching their
brothers warily.

One of the older Apache women recognizes Wright.
She nods at him as he rides past. Wright
acknowledges her with a respectful nod. Gatewood
remarks this.

GATEWOOD
Acquainted?

WRIGHT
Almost married her daughter.

Gatewood has no time for astonishment or
questions as coming forth to meet them is a
middleaged Apache with long silvery hair: CHATA.

Gatewood and Wright rein up, dismount.

Wright and Chata put arms on each other's
shoulders.

CHATA
Old friend.

WRIGHT
I won't forget this kindness.
 (nodding at him)
Lt. Gatewood.

CHATA
They call me Chata. My white name, I
cannot pronounce.

GATEWOOD
 (shaking hands)
Your chief is a very great warrior.

CHATA
You may have come for nothing. Victorio
agreed to see you, that is all. He hates
white people with all his strength. And
after them--black.

EXT. PLOWFIELD - DAY

In the broiling, burning sun, a YOUNG SUTLER is
suffering in the heat, looking for shade that doesn't
exist. Sweating profusely. But what he sees he can't
tolerate--

YOUNG SUTLER
No, no no!

The object of his displeasure: a middle-aged Apache
who is trying to hoe a furrow--with the blunt end.

The young sutler hurries to correct the errant
Apache, grabs the hoe, flips it, THUNKS it angrily
and forcefully into the blunt earth--as much as the
hard desert ground will allow.

YOUNG SUTLER
That's how you do it. It's like a knife.

The Apache doesn't seem to get it. In b.g. are others
of the tribe, young and old alike. Looking equally
mystified.

Gatewood, Wright and Chata note this scene as
they pass by.

GATEWOOD
Potatoes? In this desert?

WRIGHT
Indian Bureau orders. Last year it was
tomatoes.

CHATA
We'd be good farmers if they let us grow
cactus and sagebrush.

ON VICTORIO

The warrior chief is proud, fierce as his reputation
as the greatest leader before Geronimo. His spirit is
not broken, and he'll have nothing to do with the
scene taking place behind him. He is sitting alone
on a rock, motionless, brooding, looking at the
mountains in the East. Standing near him, acting
one concludes as bodyguard, is the strong young
WARRIOR seen earlier.

Chata explains as they come up.

CHATA
White men call them the Mimbres
Mountains. He calls them home.

Chata greets Victorio in Apache, indicates the
visitors. The chief doesn't turn or change
expression.

GATEWOOD
Tell Victorio, I know the pain in his
heart.

For answer, Victorio spits. The liquid SIZZLES as it
lands on the sunbaked rock.

Gatewood tries again.

GATEWOOD
If he will help me, maybe I can help
him.

Chata translates. This time the response is--no response.

Chata launches into a persuasive discourse, but as it ends, the effect is the same--nothing. Chata shrugs.

Wright takes matters into his own hands.
WRIGHT
Tell him, he owes me.

Chata looks at him a long moment before turning to the chief, translating. The words impact. Victorio turns around, faces them for the first time. He grunts some words in Apache and Chata:

CHATA
He says, you want to know Apache way,
prove you are Apache.

Wright understands, purses his lips. Gatewood doesn't understand, so Wright explains.

WRIGHT
He's challenging us to a race. Long distance.

GATEWOOD
I ran marathons at West Point.

WRIGHT
Sir, this isn't--

GATEWOOD
We accept.

MOMENTS LATER

Gatewood is stripping down in preparation for the
race. Wright watches.

WRIGHT
Apaches don't get tired, Lieutenant.
When they're four they're made to run
up and down cactus mountains, dry-
mouthed and naked. And when they're
done, they do it again. Backwards. Four
years young.

Gatewood takes off his boots. Looks over at his
opponent: the fierce Apache brave, who is drinking
from a gourd of water.

GATEWOOD
I grew up running in potato fields.
About the same.

WRIGHT
(nods, humoring
his superior officer)
Yes sir.

GATEWOOD
Don't take this as an order, sergeant,
but I'd like to hear about her.

Wright looks at him, realizes from Gatewood's
expression that he's sincere.

WRIGHT
We'd been chasing Victorio all over hell.
Maybe he got homesick. She knew a
little English, so she came in to parley.
After a while she started wondering if

black people could talk, 'cause all I
could do was stare at her. Never saw a
woman so good-looking, before or since.
After the truce, we took to seeing each
other.
 (hands Gatewood a canteen)
If I were you sir, I'd drink it all.

Gatewood starts to do so.

WRIGHT
It was a good time. I can't shake what I
am, and she never wanted me to.
Thanks to her, I got to know what it was
like--love. If the world just've had us
two, we'd have been fine. But you got to
live in the world there is. Where could
we run? Her people wouldn't stand for
it. Me. People can learn, I believe that,
but for some it takes time. We didn't
have enough. She never said nothing,
but I suppose they gave her so much
pain--there's a canyon in the Mimbres.
She's down there somewhere. I went
crazy for awhile, wasn't good for much.
After I got over the hate, Army took me
back. I thank 'em for that.

A SHORT TIME LATER

Wright and Gatewood walk to where the stalwart
Apache Warrior waits to begin the race. Gatewood
wears just his Army trousers, rolled up to the knee.

WRIGHT
You like whiskey, lieutenant?

GATEWOOD
Hate it. Makes me puke.

Wright gives him a look that is meant to say, this
isn't looking good.

WRIGHT
First part of the race is for bragging
rights. Second part, up that hill.

Gatewood looks in the direction Wright nods
toward.

"That hill" is a cactus-studded height, less than a
mountain but considerably more than a molehill.
On a cool day it would be a hell of an effort to go up
and down, running walking or crawling. Today isn't
that.

WRIGHT
Third part, make it back here first.
Fourth--

They remark the Warrior. He's taken a bottle of
whiskey from Chata, leans head back, chugs a big
gulp--but doesn't swallow. His cheeks bulge.

Chata tosses the bottle to Gatewood.

WRIGHT
You swallow, you lose.

Victorio stands with Chata, watching. Gatewood
knows there's no recourse, even if he wanted one.

GATEWOOD
Any other little surprises for me,
sergeant?

He takes a big gulp of the whiskey. Grunts, but the whiskey rolls around in his mouth.

WRIGHT
Yes sir.

Gatewood turns to him, surprised. Wright has stripped to the waist (but doesn't remove his suspenders).

Victorio and Chata look stunned as well.

WRIGHT
I pace him hard, maybe I can tire him out.

Gatewood can't object for the whiskey. He hands the bottle to Wright who takes a big gulp himself.

MOMENTS LATER

Chata draws a line in the dirt with the edge of his bow, then hefts it, loads an arrow, aims high--

The (now) three runners are poised in a line: the young lieutenant, imposing Apache Warrior, aging Buffalo Soldier. Chata releases the arrow. It zooms high and forward--

--and two runners SPRINT toward where they estimate from the trajectory it will fall. The third-- Wright--chugs behind, no antelope.

WITH THE WARRIOR AND GATEWOOD

Running head to head. Neither man can outswift the other.

THE ARROW

arches down, pulled by irresistible gravity--

--and HITS THE SAND simultaneously as TWO
PAIRS OF RUNNERS' FEET run past beside.

ANOTHER ANGLE

Gatewood and the Warrior head toward the granite
rock, sand and cactus outcrop that is their race
course.

ANOTHER ANGLE ON THE ARROW

As a pair of black feet pass where it is embedded in
the sand.

THE RACE - INTERCUTTING ALL THE PRINCIPALS

The Warrior picks his way over the scree, through
cactus and brush and rock with steady stride,
rhythm gained from lifelong habit.

He takes the lead.

Gatewood works harder. Frequently he breaks
stride. HEAR his BREATHING becoming labored.
Behind, Wright is sweating, but he's older than the
other two. His lope doesn't slacken and the gap
between him and Gatewood doesn't widen. He
keeps coming, sure as the desert sun that bakes
earth relentlessly.

Gatewood blinks, but this does nothing to clear the
perspiration on his face.

As the Warrior runs, still not slowing, suddenly he pulls his knife, flings it--

And as he runs past, we see a RATTLER impaled in the sand.

Now the men must climb. The pace slows. The wind picks up as they gain altitude.

They hit a talus slope. And the heat here, higher, is even fiercer.

Up they go on the slanting, loose shale rock that shifts and dislodges with every step, so that the runner below must not only avoid falling rocks become lethal by force of gravity, but also find footing.

Gatewood groans from the effort, tries to retain the whiskey.

SHOTS of the men climbing, trying to run.

The Warrior reaches the peak first.

WITH VICTORIO

Down below, Chata informs his chief. Victorio nods.

The Warrior runs past Gatewood, rather, slides-- going fast, almost slaloming.

Gatewood gives an extra effort--he's losing and won't accept it. He pumps his legs. Arrives at the top and immediately plunges down past Wright.

Below, Chata watches intently as now Wright reaches the summit. He gives this information to Victorio, who seems only a trifle less impassive at this news.

AT THE SUMMIT

Wright pauses, but he's not admiring the view--or is he? For sure, he's marshaling his strength for the descent, the only one of the runners to do so. He breathes slow, steady.

Down below his two competitors are becoming smaller and smaller to view.

Suddenly Wright heads down too. STAYING with him a moment--he's going fast, faster than his young opponents.

GATEWOOD

is pushing hard, closing the gap on the Warrior, who looks back, sees Gatewood gaining--picks up his pace.

And suddenly Gatewood runs square into a CHOLLA CACTUS. He halts. Three huge burrs of the feared "jumping cactus" are lodged in his thigh.

Gatewood reaches down to pull out the thorns--a hopeless task. Each barb, pronged at the imbedded end, pulls flesh, but Gatewood can't grip them all. The balled spikes would only imbed then in his hand.

He grimaces, virtually helpless, the pain too bad to keep on.

Wright comes up, sees what's happened and doesn't hesitate. He removes his bandanna, drapes it over the cholla burrs, grabs a piece of wood and just KNOCKS them off with a series of blows.

Gatewood's eyes shut, he flinches, tries not to swallow--

Wright's stratagem does the trick--no more cholla. Gatewood exhanges nods with his benefactor, then turns and follows Wright who suddenly sprints away--after the Warrior.

WITH WRIGHT

The finish line is still a ways off and it's crazy to sprint, but that's just what he's doing, running down the Warrior with all he's got.

INTERCUT

The Warrior is astonished to see the older man gaining, pushing him before a smart runner would, but he picks up the pace. Harder.

Wright has got a full head of steam, and he's hellbent for leather. He keeps coming as fast as he can, and the amazed Warrior has to respond--going faster and faster, staying ahead--but just.

Behind, Gatewood picks up the pace too--
Wright moves abreast of the Warrior--passes him!

VICTORIO

climbs onto a rock, the better to see. He's excited now. Other villagers are starting to crowd around to see the finish.

The Warrior is running for his people--he turns on everything he has, and that's enough to regain the lead. He passes Wright and maintains a length lead.

Up ahead they see the finish line, but can they reach it before their hearts burst?

Gatewood sees it too. Now he turns it on, and he has saved his best for last. He quickly closes the gap on the exhausted men just ahead.

Victorio for the first time shows emotion. He YELLS encouragement to the Warrior, who with guts and glorious effort pulls further ahead of Wright--

--who gives it his all and pulls abreast again, just as

Gatewood comes on.

And for a moment all three men are NECK AND NECK, heading toward the now animated, even cheering reservation Apaches--

Wright falls back, spent.

Gatewood and the Warrior come on. It's just a few meters now.

Victorio shouts again!

But it's hope lost in the wind as suddenly the Warrior collapses, falls to the sand, heaves in exhausted agony. As Gatewood surges past, the Warrior vomits amber whiskey onto the white sand.

Gatewood crosses the finish line marked in the dirt by Chata almost before the others can react to the Warrior's fall and defeat.

Gatewood heads over to the small fire prepared for just this purpose, leans down--

Spits. Nothing comes.

Gatewood tries again. Still nothing. His mouth is dry.

Again. Gatewood sputters--

A small gob of spittle--

And suddenly WHOOSH! The fire bursts into flame, doused with the alcohol spat by none other than

WRIGHT

who's crossed the finish line unnoticed by everyone. He's panting, gasping, but he's carried--and kept in his mouth--every bit of the whiskey.

Gatewood is so tired he can hardly react. He looks back and Wright follows his gaze.

The Apache women are helping the bedraggled Warrior to his feet.

Victorio and Chata are staring at Wright, just as amazed as Gatewood.

WRIGHT
Y'all never picked cotton in Arkansas.

EXT. EDGE OF TOWN - DAY

Bodney comes up to Harris.

HARRIS
No sign?

Bodney shakes his head.

HARRIS
Let's keep looking. That boy's heading
for trouble in a big hurry.

Bodney nods, head off. Harris heads in another
direction.

ANOTHER ANGLE

Harris' route takes him beside a stream at the edge
of town. As he draws closer he notes a group of
BLACK WOMEN washing clothes in the stream.

In particular he notes a young girl--MISSILOU--
among them. Harris detours their way.

HARRIS
Afternoon, ladies.

They respond with "hellos," etc. Missilou--toward
whom Harris is all eyes--just smiles. Harris moves
closer. Missilou's hair is bundled up in a plain
cloth, her face is begrimed, her clothes
nondescript--but he sees just enough to suspect
she might be pretty indeed.

HARRIS
My name's Harris. Private Harris. Of the
U.S. Cavalry. A Buffalo Soldier.

Missilou giggles. He is leaning down and sideways, trying to get a better look at her features.

HARRIS
Bet you look pretty as a button 'neath all that dirt and washcloth.

MISSILOU
(giggling)
I'll never tell.

HARRIS
I wish you would. Er, you been out here long?

MISSILOU
Two months.

HARRIS
(peering intently)
Been spending a lot of time in the sun?

WOMAN
Come on, girl.

The other women have finished their wash and are leaving. Missilou jumps up, gathers her wash.

HARRIS
(to the women)
Hey, we got a conversation going here.

Missilou hurries after them.

HARRIS
(to Missilou)
What's your name?

MISSILOU
Missilou.

HARRIS watches his quarry disappear.

HARRIS
Shit.

INT. BOWMAN'S FATHER'S LODGE - DAY

ON BOWMAN'S FATHER

an older gentleman with long white hair, an
imposing appearance, and a mischievous gleam in
his eye.

Just now he is handing an elaborately carved,
ornate pipe to Wood. WIDENING OUT, we see Sam
Bowman, sitting on the other side of the lodge.

BOWMAN
Friendship pipe.

BOWMAN'S FATHER
Friendship!

Wood's eyes widen at the size of the pipe, but he
takes it and starts puffing.

WOOD
What's in this?

BOWMAN
Strong mix.

WOOD
Yeah.

Wood lowers the pipe. Bowman's father reaches over, lifts it back to his lips.

BOWMAN'S FATHER
Friendship!

Wood puffs some more--vigorously. Clouds of smoke rise up.

Wood glances toward the other corner of the lodge, where kneels BOWMAN's SISTER, a demure woman with downcast eyes.

WOOD
Your sister talks less than you do.

She GIGGLES. Wood grins--somewhat goofily, as the pipe is getting to him--but then he notices Bowman smiling mischievously.

BOWMAN
She search husband.

He gestures toward her as if she's his for the taking. Wood's eyes widen. He looks at Bowman's father. He is smiling as well.

WOOD
Uh--

But before he can say more his head gently slumps down. The pipe slips from his grasp. He has passed out.

His father casts a reproachful look at Bowman. Sam just shrugs.

INT. TOWN SALOON - DAY

ANGLE ON BARTENDER

serving drinks to two customers at the end of the
bar, then moving toward the other end, wiping the
bar's surface with a cloth. As he nears the end he
sees what is for him an odd sight: a black man's
hands resting on the bar.

He looks up, sees Burley. He is looking admiringly,
almost astonished, at the saloon decor.

BURLEY
Real brass. Velvet. Got to be some gold
in that chandelier. Some deecor you got
here.

The bartender nervously eyes the whites at bar and
saloon.

BARTENDER
Now son, you know
better--

BURLEY
(nodding at
white patrons)
My money's green, same as theirs.

He drops his rifle PLUNK on the bar. This has an
effect. The bartender reluctantly puts a half empty
bottle of whiskey on the bar in front of Burley. He
lovingly pours himself a drink.

BURLEY
Look at that fine brown. I'm used to
gutbuster, piss yellow.

The two white men at the bar take the occasion to discreetly walk past him, exit the bar.

Burley notes their leaving but doesn't let it dissuade him from downing the shot.

He smiles with pleasure.

BURLEY
Tastes even better'n it looks.

Burley turns toward the table where four men have halted their poker game to watch him. Burley takes the whiskey, moves toward them.

AT THE TABLE

he sits, pulls from his pocket a deck of cards, FLAPS it.

BURLEY
Gentlemen, I crave a game of skill and chance.

They stare at him.

Burley pours himself another drink, begins shuffling the cards. One by one, the four men push back their chairs, stand up, walk away from the table--and out of the saloon.

Burley's smile fades to grim loneliness as he's left with nothing to play but solitaire. After a moment, he downs the drink.

EXT. TOWN STREET - DAY

A three-piece BAND has just concluded a rousing
ditty to APPLAUSE from a CROWD of the town's
citizens gathered in front of a slightly elevated
platform. The makeshift dais is comprised, besides
the band, of a few influential townsfolk and the
MAYOR, who steps forward to address the crowd.

Above him a banner proclaims the town's
anniversary festival.

MAYOR
Well friends, I don't have to tell you how
happy I am to be here again to celebrate
our fair town's founding. Especially
when I look out at you and don't see a
bunch of Comancheros.

A burly man in the front rank of the crowd, BEN,
seizes the moment--

CITIZEN
No thanks to the U.S. Army!

MAYOR
Now Ben, we're not here to--

Suddenly a COMMOTION. It's Burley--guiding his
horse directly into the crowd, scattering citizens
willy-nilly--
--and UP ONTO THE STAGE.

The astonished mayor and dignitaries scramble out
of hooves' way as Burley's horse, a little spooked by
the shouts and movement, spins nervously all over
the stage. Burley hops off the horse, staggers. He
makes no effort to control the animal.

MAYOR
(to Burley)
You gone crazy, boy?

The horse rears. The mayor lurches back, trips,
falls.

Furious, Ben jumps onto the stage and runs to help
the mayor up as two other men grab the reins, hold
Burley's horse still. Burley stands at the dais,
unsteady.

BURLEY
I'm--Buff Sojur--Buff--

BEN
He's drunk!

MAYOR
That beats it.

BEN
(to the crowd)
You want to know why
John Loco runs wild? Take a look.

Burley starts tottering, struggles to keep his
footing.

The crowd rumble with derision and laughter.

ANGLE ON HARRIS

with Bodney and the others, at a distance. Alerted
by the sound of the crowd, they spot Burley. They
hurry forward.

BEN
We knew the 9th cavalry was a
worthless bunch. Now we know they're
drunks.

Ben reaches down into the crowd, grabs a beer
from one of his friends.

BEN
Here boy, drink up.

He pours the foaming beer over Burley's head. A
ROAR of approval and laughter from the crowd.

Burley stands there for a moment, the suds
pouring down his face--

--then punches his tormentor smack in the face.

Ben falls backward, off the dais into the crowd.

There is a hush, the crowd stunned by what they
have seen-- then two men rush Burley. He punches
them both.

The crowd rushes toward the stage to get at Burley,
but suddenly--

HARRIS

and the others appear. They form a protective wall
in front of Burley. Unarmed, they just hold their
hands up.

The crowd halts--but they continue to hurl epithets
at the soldiers and Burley. In their faces we see the
rage.

BURLEY

blearily eyes this standoff—and suddenly from
behind he's POUNDED by a rifle butt. He collapses,
unconscious.

ANGLE ON SHERIFF

who has wielded the rifle, standing above Burley.

EXT. REAR OF GATEWOOD'S QUARTERS - DAY

Gatewood's sister NAN is being wooed by Lt.
SMITH.

SMITH
Bet you've had a lot of men come
courtin'.

NAN
Some.

SMITH
Yeah. Back where you come from, all
they've got to do is say "Nan Gatewood,"
and you can hear a hundred hearts
breaking.

NAN
None of them had your eloquence, Lt.
Smith.

SMITH
 (smiling cockily)
Slim pickings around here, though.

He leans closer, trying to press what he sees as his
advantage.

SMITH
Till we rode in.

NAN
Could be you'll just ride out tomorrow.

SMITH
And leave this war to a bunch of
pickaninnies? No chance.

He leans in for a kiss but abruptly stops, seeing
Gatewood and Wright have appeared, weary and
trail dusty, just now returned from San Carlos.
Gatewood is glaring.

GATEWOOD
You've got a lot to learn, mister.

Lt. Smith is nonplussed, especially at sight of
Sergeant Wright, but before he can try to extricate
himself, Harris comes up. He looks anxious,
hurried.

HARRIS
Lieutenant, sergeant.
A word with you, sirs.

INT. JAIL CELL - DAY

Burley is behind bars, bruised from his capture.
Sullen. Staring out the window.

BURLEY
What are we fighting for?

He turns, faces Wright who is standing outside the
cell confronting him.

BURLEY
Huh? Why are we getting ourselves
killed? It's not for respect. These people
don't care about us. We could bring
John Loco's head in on a stick, know
what they'd say? "Good work boy, now
here, clean my shithouse." Where's the
pride in that, sergeant? Maybe Jones is
better off. He was like a little brother to
me. I was always there, helping him out
of trouble. Wasn't any way I could keep
him out of the Army, though. He was on
fire. All I could do was tag along, like a
good big brother, watching out for him.
(a beat) Some job I did.

WRIGHT
Jones wouldn't have cared what those
people thought. His pride came from
inside, where it should. He was a brave
man who did his duty. Some day I
promise you, that's what they'll
remember. White, black, red man too.

BURLEY
I'll be long dead before that day comes.

WRIGHT
You want respect, you got to deserve it.
Stumble down drunk. Sure they
laughed at you. I'd have laughed too. A
man can't handle grief, he ain't a man.
Let me tell you something. Sure they
send us into hell, but it's not just 'cause
they call us niggers. It's cause we're
good. We do the jobs they can't. And I'll
tell you another thing. Bad as it gets,
it's better than what we came from.

BURLEY
It's too late. Leave me be.

INT. SHERIFF'S OFFICE - DAY

Gatewood is confronting the sheriff, who sits impassively behind his desk.

SHERIFF
He assaulted a white man.

GATEWOOD
Under extreme provocation.

SHERIFF
The way I saw it, he was the one got violent.

Gatewood stares long and hard at him, trying to decide whether to argue further. Instead:

GATEWOOD
What's the bail?

SHERIFF
Lieutenant, let me set you straight. It's all right by me if you let these boys do your dirty work, play soldier and all that. But when they step out of line in my town, they don't have any rights. That includes bail.

GATEWOOD
I suppose this is what's called frontier justice.

SHERIFF
He's lucky we didn't hang him.

GATEWOOD
But you will, won't you, sheriff?

SHERIFF
Have to ask you to leave, Lieutenant.
  (as Gatewood straightens up)
Take that other one with you. The two
of them together, they're stinking up my
jail.

Gatewood glares but the sheriff has turned his
attention to papers on his desk.

INT. BARRACKS - NIGHT

The usual ribbing and camaraderie are absent.
Long faces abound. A SERIES OF SHOTS shows
some men glum, others occupying themselves,
without much enthusiasm, with cleanup chores,
others just lounging.

BODNEY

is lying on his bunk when a thought occurs to him.
He begins a bluesy rendition of "Camptown Races."
But after a moment stops. He notices all the men
are staring glumly at him. Right now no one
relishes music.
Bodney replaces the harmonica under the pillow.

EXT. SAN CARLOS INDIAN RESERVATION - DAY

An ESTABLISHING SHOT of the reservation near
the general store--Indians lounging about, two
members of the Apache police, a couple whites.

INT. SUTLER'S (GENERAL) STORE - DAY

Various ANGLES of hands surreptitiously pocketing provisions of food, clothing and ammo. Amid the hustle and bustle of the store the Young Sutler does not notice these thefts, though he is casting suspicious eyes around. As well he should, for among the Indians (those doing the thefts) we spot many of Washington's tribe--among them Loren and Nana.

The Young Sutler notices Loren. Aware of his scrutiny, she tries to look inconspicuous, but he comes over to her.

YOUNG SUTLER
I've seen you before.

LOREN
I live on reservation.

YOUNG SUTLER
(eyeing her sceptically)
Maybe you know a young brave named Washington.

Throughout this conversation, we see the Indians taking more provisions: including Winchester rifles, which are slipped under robes and past the eyes of the bored Apache police.
Before Loren can answer, she hears footsteps shuffling across the floor. A man is walking somewhat haltingly to a chair beside the Young Sutler. He slumps into the seat and we recognize the Indian Agent. His mouth is bandaged and it is apparent from the dried blood that has seeped through that the wound still festers.

Loren tries not to show satisfaction but:

LOREN
(nodding at the Agent)
Was he the man who fed his tongue to
the dogs?

This hits the Agent like a blow. We see the fear in
his eyes. He darts a quick glance at Nana, who has
been hovering nearby in case of trouble.

The Agent waves his arm brusquely at the Young
Sutler, meaning emphatically: drop it.

The Young Sutler scowls but turns away without
further ado.

This time Loren does react with satisfaction.

EXT. DESERT - DAY

Washington and his friend TANATA are both at the
reins of a Conestoga wagon team.

ON COMANCHERO

COMANCHERO
Aiiyyee!

It is a signal for a race to begin. Simultaneously
Washington and Tanata whip the horses with the
reins. The wagons lurch into motion.

ANOTHER ANGLE

the wagons speed across the desert neck and neck.

WASHINGTON

whips the horses furiously. He looks to the side.
Tanata is staying abreast of him.

ANGLE ON JOHN LOCO

he and his people are loading onto horses the
provisions they have stolen from the wagons.

JOHN LOCO
I want to see who wins.

He moves down closer to the race, which is coming
his way.

MOVING WITH JOHN LOCO

for a moment, then an ANGLE on a body to the side
as he passes suggests what has just happened in
the attack on the wagon train.

THE RACE

Washington stands up, alive with excitement. He
YELLS, whips the horses furiously. Tanata does the
same, but

WASHINGTON'S WAGON

crosses the imaginary finish line first. Washington
stands high, gives his victory SHOUT.

TANATA

pulls up, shakes his head.

REAR ANGLE

we notice for the first time that a man's arm is draped over the back of the wagon. Suddenly there is movement.

Tanata watches as Washington heads his way.

Suddenly a GUNSHOT catches him squarely in the back of the head. Blood spurts. He falls off the wagon.

IN THE WAGON

the injured man falls back. It has taken all his remaining strength to fire the shot.

A shadow darkens the wagon. The man looks up to see

Washington standing over him, wielding a warclub. The man SCREAMS.

ANOTHER ANGLE

as Washington brings the club down, more than once. Then, spent with rage and grief, he leans back against the wagon.

INT. COL. HATCH'S OFFICE - DAY

Col. Hatch is pointing at a map of the southwest as he addresses his assembled officers--Morrow, Smith and Gatewood among them.

COL. HATCH
After his attack on the wagon train,
John Loco headed southeast.
 (pointing)
You should know this area by now,
Major.

Morrow nods.

COL. HATCH
I will lead the 9th here. The 6th will
circle around and meet us. At some
point, we should roust him.

The officers spring into action.

INT. JAIL CELL - DAY

Burley is lying on his back. Remembering.

FLASHBACK

EXT. BURLEY'S HOME - DAY

It is no more than a shack, in the Louisiana delta.

INT. BURLEY'S ROOM

such as it is. Burley is stuffing his meager
possessions into a bag.

Burley's GRANDFATHER appears. He is a tall man,
fit and muscular for his age, with dignity about
him. He has been a slave but it has not bowed him.

GRANDFATHER
Hear you're going to join the Army.

BURLEY
That's right, Grandpa. Don't ask me
why.

GRANDFATHER
They'll take you? A colored man?

BURLEY
Must be hard up.

GRANDFATHER
Want you to have something.

He comes over, lays a gunnysack on the bed,
carefully opens it, unwraps a metallic gray, well
used derringer.

GRANDFATHER
I earned it. With hard work.

Burley picks it up, snaps it open, inspects it.

GRANDFATHER
You're a better shot than your pa or me
put together. Take it.

BURLEY
Thanks Grandpa.

GRANDFATHER
And you do your best. Like you been
taught.

BURLEY
I'll surely try.

For the first time Burley notices that tears have
welled up in his grandfather's eyes.

GRANDFATHER
The United States Cavalry. Never
thought I'd see the day. You take care of
yourself, boy. Take care.

He clasps him in a warm strong embrace.

BACK TO PRESENT

BURLEY

gets up from his bunk, goes to the window, stares
out. He sees much bustle and stirring. A trooper
gallops past.

ANGLE ON HARRIS

standing aside as the trooper rides past.

TROOPER
 (yelling to Harris)
Reveille.

Harris nods. He is carrying a bundle of provisions
he has just purchased.

BURLEY (O.S.)
Hey, Luv!

Harris turns, sees Burley at the jail window.

BURLEY
Get Sergeant Wright for me. Hurry.

Harris nods, moves away--

And a beautiful woman passes him, shaking the long tresses of hair she has just untied and let down. Harris does a double take. It's Missilou, and she is a stunning sight for his sore eyes.

Harris stops, torn between duty and love.

BURLEY
Harris!

Harris is staring after Missilou, who throws him a wide smile as she moves away

BURLEY
I saved your life, remember?

Harris nods. He turns, hurries toward the fort. Duty is stronger than love.

But not much.

HARRIS
Shit!

INT. COL. HATCH'S OFFICE - DAY

Col. Hatch is buckling on his revolver for the march. Lt. Gatewood is with him.

COL. HATCH
The man broke the law. By rights he's under civil authority. Of course, the punishment doesn't fit the offense.

GATEWOOD
Not by a long shot, sir.

COL. HATCH
I hate this animosity between black and
white. So damn primitive. When Col.
Grierson and I formed these regiments
we made a policy. The men were to be
called "troopers." Nothing else. No
distinctions except how a man does his
duty.
 (pointedly)
Use your discretion, Lieutenant.

GATEWOOD
Yes sir.

INT. JAIL - DAY

The sheriff is once again at his work. He hears
someone entering. He looks up to see Gatewood,
backed by Wright and the rest of their unit. All are
fully armed and equipped with carbines.

And they are all pointed directly at the sheriff--

--who flinches just a tad as all together, the unit
COCK the carbines. As for a firing squad.

GATEWOOD
 (firmly, even-toned to the sheriff)
Now you've got a choice.
Talk sense and set bail, or we'll blow
your goddamn head off.

ON DESK

a set of cell keys comes dropping down PLUNK.

EXT. FORT - DAY

Col. Hatch signals "Forward ho!'

ANGLE ON MORROW

waving forward his detachment, along with
Gatewood and his Apache scouts.

ANGLE ON BURLEY

riding up, joining his unit--to welcome smiles from
the other men.

Wright nods at the unit and they move forward.

HIGH ANGLE

the 6th and 9th Cavalry diverge; Morrow's
detachment spearheads the 9th, steadily moving
away from the 6th.

ACT III

EXT. DESERT - DAY

The combined regiments move slowly across a hot, dry, barren stretch of sand flats. The men have traveled some in the heat: many have kerchiefs pouched under their caps.

EXT. CAMPFIRE - NIGHT

Bodney is improvising on his harmonica while the other troopers of Wright's unit lounge about. Burley comes over beside Bodney, leans down to get an extra cup of coffee. Bodney stops, wary of Burley after his episode with Pinckney's banjo.

BURLEY
Sounds good.

He moves away. Bodney puts the harmonica to his lips, plays away.

ANGLE ON COL. HATCH, MAJOR MORROW AND GATEWOOD

as they enter the campfire circle. Sgt. Wright jumps to attention.

WRIGHT
Attention!

COL. HATCH
At ease.

Hatch pauses a moment to survey the young trooopers before him.

CO. HATCH
Men, Lieutenant Gatewood has asked to
join Major Morrow in leading a small
handpicked group of scouts and
troopers in advance of the regiment.
You'll fight like the Apache, moving
swiftly and skirmishing at will. If you
can find John Loco and occupy him,
we'll come up and close the trap. You'll
be on your own. I needn't tell you--Each
man will have to speak for himself.

WRIGHT
I'll be glad to join the party.
 (to the troops)
And you men?

He looks to them for a response.

The men exchange looks. As it happens Col. Hatch
is standing beside Pvt. Wood. Wood opens his
mouth to answer to him, for the group, but can find
no words. Col Hatch stares at him. Waits.

WRIGHT
Private Wood, sir.

No response. For once Wood is tongue tied.

Burley steps into the breach.

BURLEY
We'll do the job.

COL. HATCH
I expect you will. Godspeed, gentlemen.

He moves away.

MAJ. MORROW
We move out now.

The others move into action. Wood is standing there fielding the bewilderment of his friends

JEFFERSON
Cat get your tongue?

WOOD
(pointing at his mouth)
Too much discipline.

MORROW'S AND GATEWOOD'S DETACHMENT

hits the trail, horses' hooves pounding, armed and equipped soldiers riding hard PAST FRAME with a vengeance toward their rendezvous with John Loco.

EXT. DESERT - WAGON TRAIN SITE - DAY

ON WAGON

its canvas canopy partially torn off, the remainder flapping in the stiff wind. The wind HOWLS through the gutted wagon.

THE TROOP

moves slowly by, the horses reined to a walk. The soldiers eye the remnants of John Loco's raid in passing.

As they move past the spectral wagon and LEAVE FRAME we see in b.g. a half-dozen new cross markers stobbed above fresh graves.

EXT. MEXICAN BORDER - DAY

The troop has halted. Morrow is with Sam Bowman,
Gatewood and a group of Apache scouts.
Reconnoitering. Morrow's ever present aide-de-
camp Harris is with him as well.

MAJ. MORROW
How far are we from the border?

BOWMAN
Close.

MAJ. MORROW
Unfortunately I left my map and
compass behind.

HARRIS
No sir, got 'em right here in my
saddlebags.

As one, they stare at him for having violated an
unspoken understanding. Eventually Harris gets it,
too.

HARRIS
But I can't seem to find 'em.

MAJ. MORROW
Too bad. We'll just have to keep
following this trail.

He motions the troops forward, trailed by Harris
who looks excited by this incursion.

HARRIS
(to the trooper at his right)
Betcha all those senoritas don't dry out.

EXT. JOHN LOCO'S STRONGHOLD - DAY

ON LOREN

LOREN
Soldiers.

JOHN LOCO

for once looks slightly taken aback.

JOHN LOCO
In Mexico?
(a beat)
Many?

She shakes her head no.

EXT. DESERT - DAY

John Loco on the march, leading his combined
force of Comancheros and Apache warriors we now
see en masse for the first time. Washington and
Nana flank Loco; the others are strung out to the
side. They are in full battle regalia, carry
Winchesters. An impressive and formidable sight.

John Loco motions to a group of riders at the end of
the line. They peel off from the group. He waves to
another group of riders. They head off in the
opposite direction.

EXT. CANYON - DAY

Morrow's column on the march. In the lead are
Gatewood, Wright and some of the Apache scouts.

LONG SHOT

the column enters a wide level canyon surrounded
by cliffs.

GATEWOOD AND BOWMAN

eye the high rock walls, narrowing as they advance.
The CLIP-CLOP of their horses' hooves ECHO
ominously.

Wright eases his horse back where he is on the side
of the column, square in the middle.

GATEWOOD
Sam, what's the worst mess of trouble
you've ever been in?

BOWMAN
 (eying the cliffs)
I'm looking at it.

A man has suddenly appeared, stepping out on the
rocks at the base of the cliff at canyon's end. He
stands regally, imperiously. Washington and a
Comanchero flank him.

Morrow motions for the troop to halt.

The Buffalo Soldiers stare at this first sight of their
foe John Loco.

WRIGHT
(quietly)
That's him. John Loco.

MAJ. MORROW
(to Harris)
White flag.
Harris reaches into his saddlebags, pulls out a
white cloth, attaches it to his rifle barrel. As he
does so:

MAJ. MORROW
Lieutenant, sergeant.

He waves them forward next to him. As they
approach, Morrow edges his horse forward. Under
Harris' white flag, they lead the troop to within
speaking distance of Loco, looking down on them
from the rocks.

MAJ. MORROW
I'm Major Albert Morrow. It saddens me
to hear how many John Loco has killed.
You and your people must surrender.

John Loco's response is immediate: laughter!--a
laugh which grows into a guffaw.

Suddenly we hear more laughter from many voices
on both sides of the canyon.

ON CLIFFS

they form a natural echo chamber, and the cries of
Comanchero and Apache are REVERBERATING
around them. The soldiers look up, all around the
cliffs, trying to spot the sources of the chanting and
shouting--to no avail.

WASHINGTON
Apache scouts!

WASHINGTON

This gets everyone's attention below. John Loco has ceased his laughter. Gradually the others' laughter ceases as well.

Other Apaches and Comancheros appear on the cliff.

Washington shouts an appeal in Apache, gesturing animatedly.

When he is finished everyone looks to Sam Bowman. He replies, yelling a brief response in Apache.

His words stir the braves. They start jeering and taunting the scouts. Some emphasize their contempt by flapping their breechcloths.

WASHINGTON
They are women!

One warrior goes further. He turns around AND MOONS THE SCOUTS--to great laughter from his friends.

Bowman responds to this in Apache--a speech that goes on for a while. At his side, Wood looks on in astonishment at this uncommon display of garrulity.

When Bowman is done, the mooning warrior is so incensed he rushes for his rifle. Two Comancheros restrain him, grappling him by the shoulders. The warrior struggles mightily.

WOOD
(to Bowman)
What did you say?

BOWMAN
I called him an asshole.

JOHN LOCO
Buffalo Soldiers! Listen to John Loco.
They made you slaves. Now you fight for
them. Why? That dirty blue uniform?

This touches Burley. He regards Loco intently.

JOHN LOCO
Join me.

GATEWOOD
(to Morrow)
Permission to speak, sir.

Morrow nods.

GATEWOOD
(to Loco) John Loco distrusts us. God
knows you have good reason. We've
made mistakes. But look.

He raises up in his saddle, points to the troop.

GATEWOOD
Look at us. It's not too late to live
together peacefully.

JOHN LOCO
I speak to the Buffalo Soldiers!

This time everyone looks to Wright. He waits before
replying.

He turns in saddle, stares at his men. No need to
say a word. They all know he's searching for any
sign of doubt.

He reserves a longer look for Burley.

There is no change of expression on the private's
face.

Wright turns back to face Loco. He shakes his
head. Loco looks grim.

JOHN LOCO
Fools.

He leaps off the ledge, disappears into the rocks.
Washington and the others do likewise.

The Comancheros and warriors disappear from the
cliffs.

Silence.

Harris takes the white cloth from his gun.

MAJ. MORROW
 (to Harris)
Well private, pretty soon you'll see all
the combat you want. I imagine you're
pleased.

HARRIS
(deadpan)
Overjoyed, Sir.

They hear a SOUND—

THEIR POV

Thundering over a rise at the head of the canyon behind them, appearing in view with a terrifying abruptness, are John Loco's Comancheros and warrior band in a fierce charge.

INTERCUT COMANCHEROS AND SOLDIERS

The Comancheros roar forth, riding full speed.

MAJ. MORROW
Dismount!

The soldiers with rapid precision get off their horses, kneel in units.

The Comancheros open up with their Winchesters.

MAJ. MORROW
Commence firing!

Burley, Wood and the others fire back with their carbines. A brace of Comancheros are hit.

The line of riders onslaughts--

Burley ducks a rider by diving aside--bullets SPATTER the ground in his wake--then pulls his revolver and shoots the rider from behind.

A MELEE

as the two groups collide in combat.

SERIES OF SHOTS

--Comancheros going down.

--Several troopers hit.

--A brave wielding a warclub battering a trooper as he roars past, but Wright leaps, pulls him off his horse. Wright wrenches the warclub away, uses it on the brave.

—John Loco and Washington are firing round after round from the rocks above. We see three troopers go down from their shots.

As the Comanchero charge finally moves past:

MAJ. MORROW
Take cover!

The troopers mount--those whose horses have not scattered. Wood has to grab his rearing horse's reins and pull him down.

As Morrow mounts he notices a lone Comanchero on the ground, firing away in the maelstrom of troopers and Comancheros. The Comanchero is directly in line with the rocks where Morrow intends to take cover.

Morrow spurs his horse into a gallop. In one swift ride he grabs a Winchester by the barrel from a Comanchero, rips it from his hands. Then swinging the rifle like a polo mallet he charges--

As the Comanchero takes aim at Burley, Morrow swings the Winchester, knocks the Comanchero's rifle out of his hands.

ANGLE ON JOHN LOCO

firing at him.

MORROW

is hit. He falls off his horse before he can reach the protecting rocks.

Around him two horses are hit and tumble down. Other troopers fall, hit by the withering barrage of fire from Loco and his men above.

Wood's horse is shot and falls, but he manages to leap off, get up and scramble for the rocks.

HARRIS

sees Morrow down. He spurs his horse toward him.

A dismounted Comanchero takes aim at Morrow. As Harsis thunders past, he guns him down with a revolver shot.

Morrow rises unsteadily to his feet, clutching his wounded left side. Harris scoops him up on the dead run, carries him side-horse toward the rocks.

Reaching them, Harris deposits the Major in the hands of the troopers, who hustle him out of harm's way. Morrow grimaces as he is laid behind a rock.

HARRIS

turns back to the fight but he is hit--once, twice.
His horse rears back and away.

MAJ. MORROW
Get him!

Wood and Burley move out but a barrage of fire
prevents them from going further--and by now the
horse is cantering away, the wounded Harris
clinging to the reins. Harris just slumps over in the
saddle. His undirected horse drifts back and forth,
away slowly from the crossfire toward the end of
the canyon. A grim Morrow turns to Gatewood.

MAJ. MORROW
Got to get word to the rest of the
regiment.

GATEWOOD
Yessir. But we're cut off.

He and the others eye their predicament. They're
under cover but John Loco and his men are above
and directing a blistering fire toward them, the
bullets PINGING off the rocks.

GATEWOOD
Can't get a rider through that.

Wright and Gatewood exchange looks.

WRIGHT
I've got an idea.

GATEWOOD
Same as mine?

They nod to each other, then turn as one.

WRIGHT & GATEWOOD
Private Wood!

A SHORT TIME LATER

ON WOOD

straightening his bandolier, tucking in his pants,
preparing for a mission. Wright is hovering around
him, as is Sam Bowman. Wright has Wood's hat in
his hand.

WOOD
You wear it, sarge. It'll bring you good
luck.

Wright looks at it, winces.

WRIGHT
Better you.

He hands it back.

BOWMAN
(to Wood)
Good luck.

WOOD
(exasperatedly)
I'm about to get myself killed. Reduced
to my scalp. Once in your life you might
say a little more than that.

Bowman thinks a moment.

BOWMAN
Godspeed.

LATER

Wood runs downhill through a boulder field,
dodging fire, till he gets to the edge of the troopers'
flank.

The troopers watch him go, realizing their lives may
be riding on his success.

Wood gets on his stomach, starts crawling around
boulders, trying to hide his presence and
movements.

WRIGHT
Let's make some noise.

He leads a barrage of fire. Bullets riddle the
Comancheros' positions, causing some to duck
behind cover.

MORROW

is being bandaged by Jefferson. He winces as
Jefferson does his work.

BURLEY

notices Harris' horse is edging toward the
Comanchero side of the canyon. Burley dashes
down to get a closer viewpoint.

Wood notices a COMANCHERO moving toward
Harris' horse. Wood grimaces.

INTERCUT COMANCHERO, HARRIS AND BURLEY

the horse gets closer. The Comanchero reaches for the reins

BURLEY FIRES.

The shot shatters the Comanchero's hand. He falls back, screaming in pain, clutching his hand.

The horse rears, canters away. Toward Wood who quickly crawls and scrambles his way down, up and around a shallow ravine, then wiggles the last few yards.

ANOTHER ANGLE

he cautiously raises his head up. The horse is a few feet away. Wood reaches his hand out.

WRIGHT
More music!

A fusillade from the troopers batters the Comancheros' position, providing a cover fire for Wood.

Just as Wood is about to grasp the reins, the horse picks its head away. Wood mutters a curse.

Burley, watching, curses likewise at Wood's near miss.

JOHN LOCO

senses something amiss. He moves down in the rocks for a better view.

WOOD

the horse is a few feet away, so close yet so far.
Wood tenses, ready to chance a suicidal dash for
the horse.

ANGLE ON HARRIS'S HAND

tugging the reins--edging his horse toward Wood.

WOOD

looks up as the horse approaches.

JOHN LOCO

sees what's going on, barks out an order. Two
warriors raise rifles.

HARRIS

looks down at WOOD.

HARRIS
 (struggling to muster words)
Got a horse for you, trooper.

Suddenly Harris is battered in the back by a volley
of GUNSHOTS. The force of the bullets literally
knocks him out of the saddle. Wood catches him,
cradles him in his arms, sets him down gently.

HARRIS
I'm done. Ride him, son.

Wood nods. The horse rears, bullets SPATTERING
around.

Wood leaps into the line of fire, grabs the reins and vaults into the saddle. He jerks the horse around and lashes him into a gallop.

Wood rides!

The Comancheros rain a hailstorm of bullets toward the fleeing rider.

But he's outrunning them. The Buffalo Soldiers direct a
protective crossfire.

Wood whips his horse toward the end of the canyon. Suddenly a Comanchero appears, stationed at canyon's end by John Loco for just such a trick. He calmly takes aim with his Winchester as Wood bears down on him, squeezes the trigger.

BURLEY

fires first.

THE COMANCHERO

is blasted out of Wood's way by Burley's shot. Wood blazes PAST FRAME where the Comanchero had stood.

JOHN LOCO

signals--

Four COMANCHERO HORSEMEN ride off in pursuit of Wood.

Seeing this, Burley and the others unleash fire
toward them.

No luck.

The horsemen escape out of range and head off in
pursuit of Wood.

Burley mutters "Damn."

ANOTHER ANGLE

there is a sudden lull, as if both sides are
contemplating Wood's hair-raising escape. All is
quiet, till John Loco's voice is heard, reverberating,
ECHOING off the cliffs to eerie effect.

JOHN LOCO
If he makes it, what then? I've sent men
to lead your friends astray. Your rider
will find old trails. Nothing more.

Coming as it does with the intensified impact of
silence, his words hit the soldiers with extra
impact.

WOOD'S RIDE

Various ANGLES show Wood and his steed
blistering the desert sand, plunging up and over
dunes, leaping draws, outpacing the pursuing
riders.

One of the pursuers snaps off a shot from his
Winchester--misses.

Wood reins up. Ahead lies a deep arroyo. Wood
takes a look back at his pursuers, spurs his horse
forward.

ARROYO

Wood sends his mount SOARING over the arroyo.

WOOD
Whoo!

The Comanchero fires again--and Wood's horse is
hit just as it lands on the other side. Horseman and
rider go crashing down. Wood lies motionless.

The Comancheros ease their horses down the
embankment of the arroyo.

WOOD

shakes his head, trying to clear it. He struggles up,
groggy, stumbles over to his horse. Blood streams
from the horse's head.

The Comancheros appear, riding pell-mell toward
him. Wood pulls his revolver, snaps off six shots.
Only one Comanchero goes down.

Wood tries to pull his rifle out of its scabbard, but the horse's full weight is on it.

ON WOOD

as the Comancheros reach him in full gallop and RIDE HIM DOWN.

EXT. MOUNTAIN PASS - DAY

ON COMANCHEROS

a half-dozen at most, stationed along the pass.

They are directing fire at a regiment pinned down in the canyon below--specifically the 6th Cavalry, more specifically Lt. Smith's regiment.

We PAN back and forth as one shot follows another--it is a scene very similar to that when Wright and Gatewood's squads were pinned down.

ANGLE ON LT. SMITH

hunkering down with a SERGEANT behind rocks as the bullets impact all around.

SERGEANT
How many you figure?

SMITH
A hundred, maybe two hundred.

The sergeant nods. No doubt his superior officer knows what he's talking about. BING! They duck precipitately as SHOTS carom off the boulder in front of them.

EXT. DESERT - ANOTHER AREA - DAY

An Apache SCOUT is eyeing a trail as Col. Hatch rides up to him, his detachment in b.g.

APACHE SCOUT
Trail leads south. Six, seven riders.

COL. HATCH
Could be a diversion.
 (a beat, looking back at the
 mountains)
Well, let's find out.

They ride OUT OF FRAME, leaving us a view of the mountains where Morrow, Gatewood and the Buffalo Soldiers are trapped.

EXT. CANYON - DAY (SUNSET)

The sun moves behind the cliff, plunging the canyon into twilight gloom.

ANGLE ON PINCKNEY

peering over a boulder.

HIS POV

PANNING the cliff--we see no sign of the Indians.

PINCKNEY
Could be they've pulled out.

Pinckney decides to test the theory. He takes a drinking cup from his mess-kit, tosses it out into the open, where it hits the ground with a CLANG.

ON DRINKING CUP

as it is punctured and battered by a dozen
GUNSHOTS from all directions.

PINCKNEY
Nope.

EXT. JOHN LOCO'S BASTION - NIGHT

Washington is twisting the string on his bow
tighter. He notices his hands are shaking slightly.

WASHINGTON
They call me a brave warrior. Yet I
tremble.

JOHN LOCO
Don't fear to die. It was worse to live as
you were. This land you used to call
yours, now you drift across like the
stormwind. Unwanted, unwelcome.
Cursed.

WASHINGTON
You think as the Apache.
 (a beat)
Father.

EXT. CANYON - NIGHT

Morrow has summoned Gatewood and Wright.

MAJ. MORROW
No telling whether the regiment will
arrive. Thoughts, gentlemen?

GATEWOOD
We're outnumbered three to one. They'll
hit us at first light.

MAJ. MORROW
I expect you're right.

WRIGHT
Sir, I have an idea. If some of our men
can sneak through, we can hit 'em in a
crossfire.

MAJ. MORROW
No good. They'll spot them for sure,
even at night.

WRIGHT
You forget, sir. Our men have an
advantage. We look like the night.

Morrow takes this in.

LATER

Burley, Jeffferson, Jordan and several others have
stripped themselves of everything flashy or light-
colored.

Wright leads the group.

WRIGHT
Ready?

Clutching knives and revolvers, the men move out.
We follow them for a moment as they creep into the
darkness.

ANGLE ON PINCKNEY

who along with Bodney and the rest have now
moved into a defensive perimeter around Morrow.
Bodney takes his harmonica, TRILLS it across his
lips. From this Gatewood gets an idea.

GATEWOOD
(loudly)
Major, I'm in the wrong outfit. The
Buffalo Soldiers I know would be having
a good time. Here, I'll show you.

He launches into a loud, very offkey version of
"Camptown Races." His rendition brings a wince
from Major Morrow--not to mention the troops.

PINCKNEY
(grimacing)
Damn.

Gatewood continues singing, gesturing for them to
join in.

PINCKNEY
I get the idea.

Realizing this is a diversion, Pinckney starts playing
the harmonica. Another trooper overturns a kettle,
starts banging it like a drum. Soon there is a
veritable chorus of "Camptown Races" echoing
through the night.

EXT. JOHN LOCO'S CAMP - NIGHT

John Loco, Washington and Nana are watching the
Buffalo Soldiers' campfire from a distance. They
can hear the chorus.

WASHINGTON
These Buffalo Soldiers <u>are</u>
different. They're crazy.

JOHN LOCO
Let them sing. They won't fool us again.

IN THE DARKNESS

VARIOUS ANGLES

of the Buffalo Soldiers slipping stealthily through
the night.

ON TWO SENTRIES

listening to the Buffalo Soldiers' SONG, gazing
toward their encampment. While they watch and
listen, Wright and Jefferson crawl past.

BURLEY

is almost discovered by a Comanchero when he
accidentally kicks a rock. But he hastily hunches
up against a rock, blending in with the darkened
hollow at the base of the rock. The Comanchero
moves closer, stares directly at him.

COMANCHERO'S POV

all he sees is the night. He moves away.

Burley waits a moment, then slips past.

DISSOLVE TO:

THE SKY

as the first shafts of light break through.

EXT. DESERT (TRAVELING) - DAY (DAWN)

ANGLE ON COMANCHERO

riding. He is wearing Wood's shirt.

ANGLE ON COMANCHERO #2

he has Wood's bandolier.

ANGLE ON COMANCHERO #3

he is wearing Wood's hat. He WHOOPS, raises it
high, swats his horse's side with it--and now we see
Wood himself, alive but strapped to the side of the
horse like big game just bagged.

The Comancheros are having a fine old time
taunting their captive. To add insult to injury,
Comanchero #3 now begins spinning his horse in a
circle. WOOD whirls like a top.

WOOD
Asshoooooooole!

The Comancheros laugh with glee, spur their
horses. Together they ride like hell toward a nearby
rise.

WOOD jounces like crazy.

As the three Comancheros mount a hillock they
rein up to a dead stop and we see why--

ANOTHER ANGLE

they are confronting THE U.S. ARMY--to wit, they
have inadvertently come face to face with Col.
Hatch and the regiment. No place to run, no place
to hide before a hundred soldiers.

Hatch eyes the Comancheros, then hears an
undaunted VOICE emanating from somewhere near
a Comanchero's horse:

WOOD
Private Wood reporting, sir.

EXT. CANYON - DAY (DAWN)

CLOSE ON JOHN LOCO

JOHN LOCO
Yiha!

His war whoop brings the Comancheros charging
onto the Buffalo Soldiers' perimeter.

SERIES OF SHOTS

--The Comancheros firing.
--The troopers, Morrow included, firing back.
--A Comanchero on the cliff above rolling down a
boulder which tumbles through the camp.
--Washington hitting a soldier with a shot.
--A group of Comancheros breaking through the
perimeter.
--From a sitting position, Morrow fires off shots.

GATEWOOD

takes matters into his own hands. Yelling madly, he
charges forward, shooting--hitting two, tackling the
others before they can fire. Pinckney comes to his
aid and they finish off the two Comancheros.

ON JOHN LOCO

satisfied with the way the battle is going for his
men--but he senses something behind and--as he
jerks around IN FRAME, his eyes widen with
astonishment at what he sees.

HIS POV

the Buffalo Soldiers, Wright's group, have rounded
up their mounts. They are in formation, carbines
ready.

WRIGHT
Charge!

They do--at full gallop. Each Buffalo Soldier takes
the reins in his teeth. After each shot, they pull a
bullet from their carabiniers, reload, fire again.

The soldiers come charging, a wild ride into the
midst of John Loco's men.

GATEWOOD
Let's go!

He waves some of his men forward. They go out to
meet the charge, crossfiring John Loco and his
men.

SERIES OF SHOTS

The fighting is fierce, at close quarters, some hand to hand. Loco kills two troopers. He is fighting alongside Washington, who is wielding a warclub.

Loco signals retreat. He and the warriors move up into the rocks.

GATEWOOD
Cover us.

He waves to Wright, Burley, Pinckney and Jefferson. They scramble up the hillside in pursuit. Below, the Buffalo Soldiers directed by Morrow kneel, direct fire above.
UP THE SLOPE

we follow the Buffalo Soldiers. Burley weaves in and out of the boulder field, keeping an eye out constantly for an ambush.

WASHINGTON

makes it to a makeshift breastwork. He turns, starts firing to devastating effect. He hits a Buffalo Soldier below, then wounds Wright.

Wright falls, clutching his shoulder.

Gatewood comes to his aid, dragging him behind a boulder.

BURLEY AND PINCKNEY

continue upward, dodging fire.

GATEWOOD

hunkers down with Jefferson and the wounded Wright. He puts Wright's revolver in his hand.

Suddenly they're hit by a charge of Comancheros. Gatewood guns down two. Wright grapples with another, rolls--kills him with a knife. In the melee Jefferson is wounded.

Fire from Gatewood drives the remaining Comancheros off.

PINCKNEY

makes it to the breastwork. Washington whirls, shoots him squarely in the face.

Pinckney tumbles down the mountain--past Burley. The sight enrages Burley. He charges upward, dashing up the slope, oblivious to the bullets impacting all around him.

ON PINCKNEY

the life gone from his face, blank eyes staring upward.

AT THE BREASTWORK

Burley leaps over it, fires as he tumbles. Washington's Winchester is hit, ricochets out of his hands.

Washington pulls a knife, flings it. It catches Burley's shoulder. He yells in pain, wrenches it out, drops his revolver.

Waving the warclub, Washington rushes forward.
Burley slips aside an instant before Washington
slams the warclub down--just missing.

Burley rolls aside as Washington swings again with
the warclub. Burley stumbles back against the
breastwork.

JOHN LOCO

some distance away, fires a shot toward him. It
slams off the rock beside Burley, who ducks again.
Washington's warclub CLANGS against the
breastwork.

Burley jabs the knife into Washington's stomach.
Against the tough muscle and skin, the blade's edge
turns, glances off--the knife slipping out of Burley's
hand.

John Loco runs to his son's aid.

Meanwhile the fighting below has reached a lull. A
Comanchero at cliff's edge has spotted something
in the distance.

GATEWOOD

satisfies himself Wright is not badly wounded.
Wright gestures to Gatewood to head up the hill.

WRIGHT
I'm all right.

Gatewood waves down below. The remaining
Buffalo Soldiers head up the hill.

Gatewood hurries upward toward Burley.

Wright spots a rifle fallen on the ground. He begins crawling toward it.

AT THE BREASTWORK

Washington swings again, and this time the warclub hits Burley's shoulder a glancing blow. Burley yells in pain, but has enough force to punch Washington who falls backward.

Burley collapses. Realizing he's virtually helpless, Washington grips the warclub, smiles. Gives his war cry.

WASHINGTON
Aiiyee!

He charges Burley for the coup de grace.

ON BURLEY'S SLEEVE

as he whips out the derringer, fires both barrels-- POP! Washington comes on, charges into Burley. They both go down.

JOHN LOCO

runs up to see them both down--

Burley pushes Washington's body off him. Blood stains Washington's forehead.

GATEWOOD

finds his charge up the hill stalled by fire from above. He has to take cover, return fire.

BURLEY

holds his injured shoulder, unable to move.

John Loco looks down at the body of his son.
Emotion shows on his face. He turns to Burley.

JOHN LOCO
My son was a great warrior. I will honor
your bravery by killing you quickly. You
understand this?

BURLEY
Understood.

He moves over to Burley. Raises his rifle, aims it
point blank at Burley--and the chamber CLICKS.
Empty.

WRIGHT

from a kneeling position below fires, guns down the
2 snipers pinning down Gatewood.

Gatewood hurries up toward the breastwork.

JOHN LOCO

looks down, sees Gatewood and, behind him,
Buffalo Soldiers coming to Burley's aid.
A YELL from the Comanchero who was standing at
cliff's edge alerts Loco.

HIS POV

dust clouds near at hand signal the approach of
Col. Hatch's regiment.

Loco's Comancheros are scrambling for their horses. Nana is leading Loco's horse his way.

John Loco bends down, lifts his son in his arms. Cradling him carefully, he carries him down to the horse Nana has waiting. Burley struggles up, looks down just as Loco mounts, his son slung over the back of the horse.

Loco gives Burley a last look.

JOHN LOCO
God smiled on the black man today.

He rides off. His Comancheros and Apache warriors thunder after him.

Gatewood arrives at the breastwork, comes up to Burley, bends over him.

GATEWOOD
He's heading toward the 6th Cav.

BURLEY
(softly)
They won't stop him.

Something draws his eye.

CLOSE ON WARCLUB AND REVOLVER

lying side by side, blood staining the ground on which they lie.

EXT. HEAD OF CANYON - DAY

Hatch's regiment arriving--

Wood, bandaged but not broken, rides near the advance guard.

EXT. JOHN LOCO'S STRONGHOLD - DAY

ON BIER

on which the body of Washington lies. A burial ceremony is in progress. Wind whips around the assembled mourners.

JOHN LOCO

stands motionless, impassive, grim. We HOLD on him for a long moment.

LOREN

is leading the Apache women in a MOURNING

TRILL.

ANOTHER ANGLE ON JOHN LOCO

now he is weeping.

INT. BARRACKS - DAY

ANGLE ON ACCORDION

lightly playing a lively tune with a Cajun beat.

WIDENING OUT, we see a new recruit, PVT. THOMAS, playing the accordion. He is sitting on the bunk formerly occupied by Jones.

ANGLE ON STOCKLEY

another new recruit, unloading gear onto Pinckney's former bed. He notes Pinckney's broken banjo has been placed like a knick-knack at the head of the bed.

STOCKLEY
(to Wright, meaning the banjo)
That thing work, Sarge?

WRIGHT
It used to.

Bodney pulls out his harmonica, joins Thomas.
They begin a duet.

BURLEY

is sitting near Wright, who is shaving, looks
recovered from his battle wound.

BURLEY
Haven't heard from Mr. John Loco in a
long time, Sarge. You reckon he's had
enough?

WRIGHT
What do you think?

BURLEY
(after a beat)
He'll be back.

Jefferson turns to Burley, who is flexing his
wounded shoulder.

JEFFERSON
Reckon he'll be looking for you.

BURLEY
The way I see it, we're square.
Don't think I can persuade him, though.

WOOD

is watching exasperatedly as a new RECRUIT mops
the barracks floor. Unable to stand it any longer, he
hops off his bunk, goes over to the recruit.

WOOD
You're making a mess.
 (taking the mop, showing him)
Got to have a logic to it. What's that big
"D" word?

RECRUIT
Discipline.

WOOD
Yeah.

He gives the mop back to the recruit, who starts
mopping more smoothly. Wood approves, then
notes something outside.

WOOD
Lot of activity out there.

Gatewood enters.

GATEWOOD
Gentlemen, parade grounds at oh-nine
hundred hours. Full dress. By order of
the colonel.

BURLEY
What's the occasion?

Gatewood has in hand one of the dress Hessian-
style helmets the soldiers wear only on special
occasions.

GATEWOOD
Kind of a ceremony.

He tosses the helmet to Burley. He and the others all eye the ornate crest.

EXT. PARADE GROUNDS - DAY

The regimental BAND begins a drumroll.

WIDENING OUT, we see Col. Hatch in foreground with an ORDERLY. In b.g. the regiment, in ceremonial dress, mounted, watches. Standing closer, officers--including Morrow and Gatewood.

COL. HATCH

steps forward in front of the regiment.

COL. HATCH
Gentlemen, for bravery and gallantry above and beyond the call of duty, a grateful nation presents you its highest military award-- the Medal of Honor.

ANGLE ON WRIGHT

as Hatch pins a medal on his chest.

ANGLE ON GATEWOOD

standing with his wife beside Major Morrow. Nan Gatewood stands with Lt. Smith, who seems to have learned , as he's properly respectful.

COL. HATCH
First Sgt. Joseph J. Wright.

WOOD
 (to Burley at his side)
"Joseph?"

Burley just smiles because now it's Wood's turn.

COL. HATCH
Corporal Tyrone Wood.

Then his.

COL. HATCH
Corporal Zachary Burley.

ANOTHER ANGLE

Burley's grandfather is there. He smiles with
happiness, and not a little surprise.

Col. Hatch does a doubletake at the last name on
his list, but there's nothing to do but say it.

COL. HATCH
Corporal Harris er, "Luv" Harris.

It is indeed Harris--leaning on a crutch, an arm still
bandaged--but alive.

Missilou stands to the side of them. She beams as
Harris gets his medal.

As Hatch pins it on:

HARRIS
Thank you, sir.

Medals pinned, Hatch raises his hand in salute.
The four honorees follow suit.

COL. HATCH
Congratulations--Buffalo Soldiers.

They exchange salutes. The regimental band strikes
up "Camptown Races."

Col. Hatch shakes hands with each man in turn.

NAN GATEWOOD

gives Lt. Smith a wry look. He smiles,
understandably abashed.

The official part of the ceremony over, the principals
disperse, greet their loved ones. Morrow and
Gatewood move among the group, shaking hands
with the Medal of Honor winners.

BURLEY

hugs his grandfather.

GRANDFATHER
(to Burley)
Lieutenant said you was a hero.

Gatewood comes up to Burley, shakes his hand.

GATEWOOD
(to Burley)
Well done.

WOOD

looks up to see Bowman, who extends his hand for
a congratulatory shake--and smiles! An even bigger
surprise to the stunned Wood--it's a wide engaging
smile.

WOOD
I don't believe it. You can smile!

BOWMAN
Smoked father's pipe.

HARRIS

is proudly showing off his medal to Missilou.

HARRIS
I ever tell you what they call me back
home?

WRIGHT

is fingering his medal, trying not so successfully to
mask the emotion he feels as Gatewood comes up
to him.

GATEWOOD
Well, sergeant. Your thoughts?

WRIGHT
 (a beat)
We've come a ways.

Other members of the troop move in to congratulate
Burley.

Bodney admires the medal.

BODNEY
How it does shine. You reckon Jones
can see it up there from the pearly
gates?

BURLEY
Yep.

He fingers the medal. It glints in the sunlight.

BURLEY
He'll be right proud.

A FINAL SHOT

the Buffalo Soldiers in perfect regimental formation
ride TOWARD CAMERA, then past.

EXT. DESERT - DAY

We watch them for a long moment, riding off, the
horses' hooves clip-clopping, the men sitting
ramrod straight in the saddle.

Soldiers riding into a history that for too long a time
will neglect, but never quite forget them.

FADE OUT:

THE END

Dedicated to the men of the 9th and 10th US Cavalry.

ACKNOWLEDGMENT

Grateful acknowledgment to Jeffry Martini for his original story suggestions and passionate efforts on behalf of this project.